DEATH BALL

by EDDIE RUZZI

ISBN 978-1-7354386-0-3 (paperback)
ISBN 978-1-7354386-2-7 (digital)

2nd Edition

Artwork by JR Hortsting

This is a work of fiction. All of the characters, names, incidents, organizations, and dialogue in this novel are either the products of the author's imagination or are used fictitiously.

Printed in the United States of America

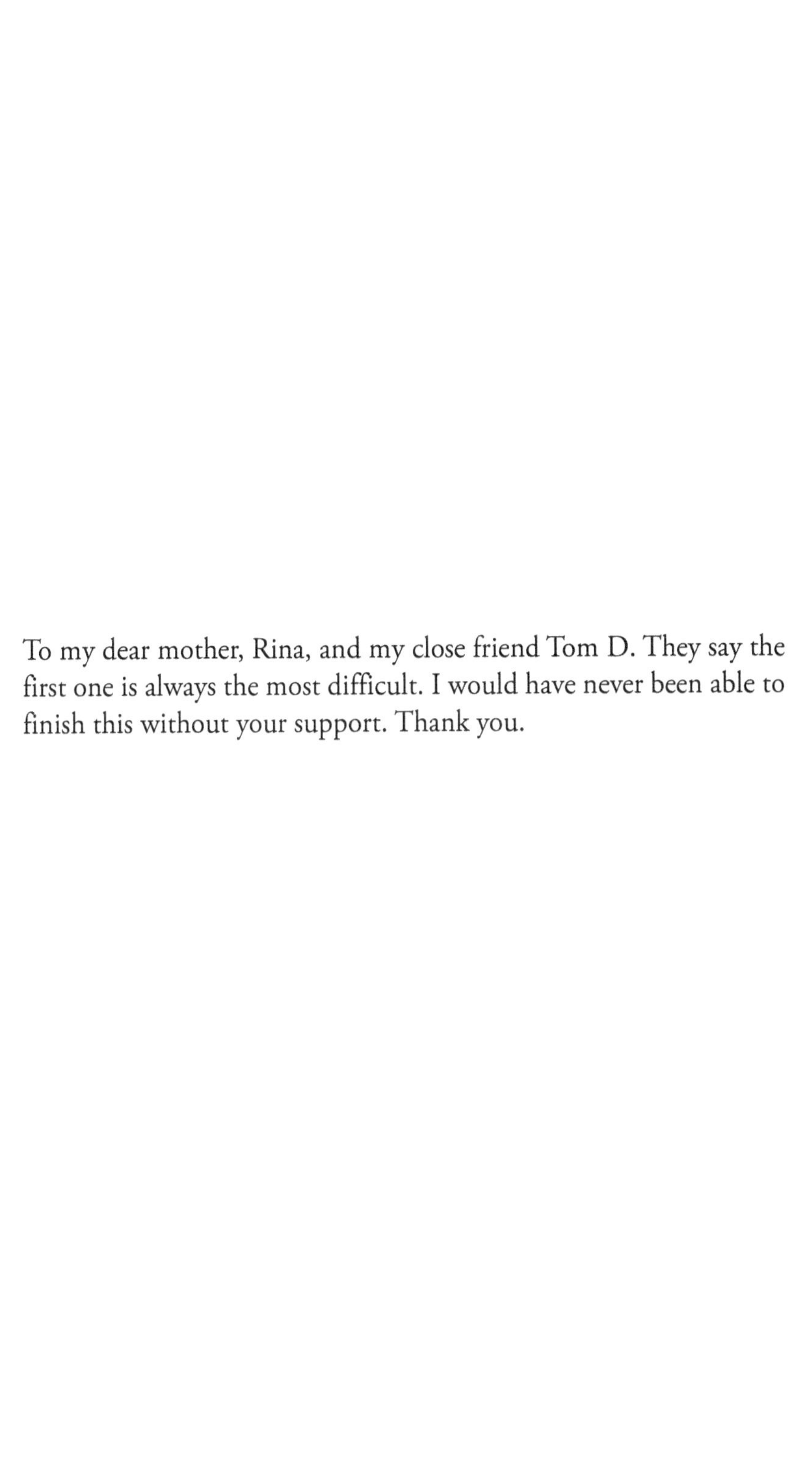

To my dear mother, Rina, and my close friend Tom D. They say the first one is always the most difficult. I would have never been able to finish this without your support. Thank you.

PACIFIC BOOK REVIEW

"A great book for Sci-Fi fans. Filled with high-octane action, deep seated mythology and a great cast of characters, readers will instantly fall in love with this thrilling adventure that is a blend of Hunger Games, Gladiator, and Star Trek."

HOLLYWOOD BOOK REVIEW

"Death Ball is an excellent mix of quick entertainment, vivid images and fun reading. Ruzzi writes in an expansive way that totally promotes sci-fi."

A NOTE FROM THE AUTHOR

Due to recent events, some readers may find certain dialects in this novel offensive. This was never my intention, but rather a way to capture the voices of the characters described for dramatic effect. I have always strived to be inclusive of, and empowering for; both women *AND* people of color in my writing. As such, I have elected not to edit these sections out, and instead inform readers in the hopes that they will understand its context.

Sincerely and respectfully,
Eddie Ruzzi

CONTENTS

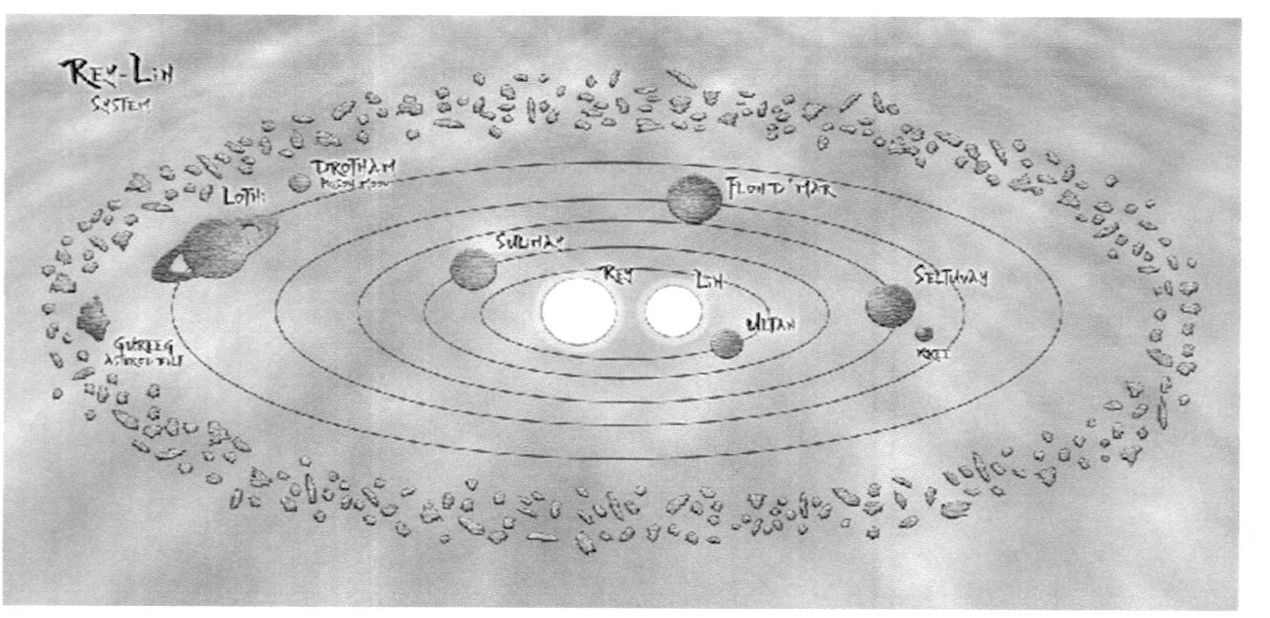

Map of Rey-Lin Solar System

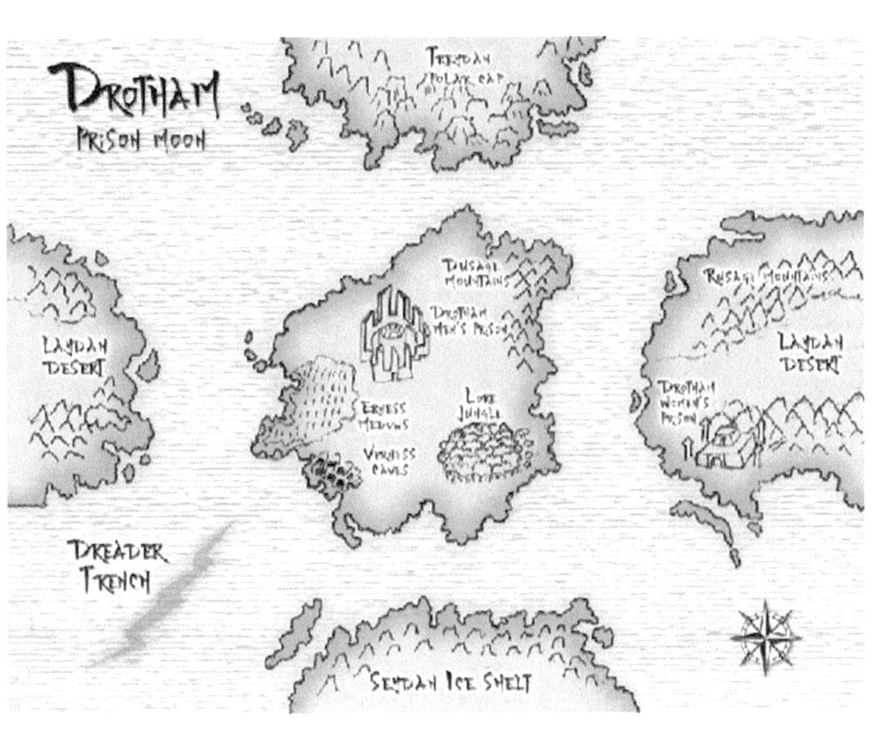

Map of Drotham Prison Moon

PROLOGUE

Two ships vie for position as they fly wildly behind a third craft. The matte-gray vehicles are identical save for different white numbers emblazoned on their sides. The pursuing shuttles train bursts of blue-white energy at the lead vessel, which is carrying a metal-plated ball nestled against its underbelly that displays red numbers counting down to zero. A large aperture—called a nulling ring—with steel plating bordering it, and a greenish-blue plasma interior, lies on the side of a mountain in front of the speeding vessels. The ship with the ball flings it at the hole but misses, sending it careening down the snowy slope. Another craft swoops in; fires a grappling claw attached to a heavy steel cable, and snatches the gray orb. The vessel pulls up hard, missing a rock outcropping by only meters while evading the other pursuers.

As the aircraft climbs, the other ships realize it can no longer retract the sphere that is now swinging below it. They unleash several salvos at the new leader. Smoke billows out of the defender's left engine while it races to drop the ball into the blinking orifice below. The shuttle lets the ball fly, but the counter reaches zero before the sphere can land in the nulling ring. It explodes with a fiery blast, consuming all three ships, and etching a massive crater into the snowy mountain slope.

There will be no *Death Ball* winner today.

THE MASSACRE ON KREE

Diffused light feigns through the opaque glass window of a cell occupied by Tosin Luval. Spying his reflection in the mirror across from his cot, deep green eyes under black, cropped hair on an angular face peer back at him as though they were from someone else. The prisoner, a major in the System Guard, the military force overseeing law and order in a binary star system named Rey-Lin, awaits his trial. Having always been in control of his life, Tosin is struck by how quickly things have turned against him. A distinguished officer who had devoted his life to the military, his present situation comes as a shock. Not even the offensive on Tal Rutette—A six-month confrontation against a group of brutal guerrilla separatists costing the lives of thousands of men, women and children—had affected him this way. He had remained unfazed while piloting a ship through withering enemy defenses to deliver a squad of Special Force commandos to the terrorist's central headquarters. The raid had ended the war, and garnered Tosin a *Dureen Award*—the highest honor in the System Guard.

The incarcerated officer leaps off his bed onto the floor in a single, fluid motion and begins a regimen of calisthenics to clear his mind. Once finished, he continues through a dizzying set of martial arts exercises. But the thoughts persist. They *said* he could get a light sentence, however the charges against him carry severe punishments, possibly death … or worse … life on the prison moon of Drotham. Tosin stops after a while and sits cross-legged on the floor. He wipes the sweat from his brow before beginning to meditate—slowing his breathing while mentally replaying the events of the past few days that led to this situation. With his hands rested on his knees, he shuts his eyes and falls into a waking dream.

Major Luval is mingling with politicians at an affair in the capital city of Solonos on the planet of Sulimay, the seat of all governmental power for the Rey-Lin system. The turquoise and dark blue colors of his uniform reveal conscription to both the hydro and space branches of the System Guard. The breast of his dress jacket resembles an exploding Kaliope due to all his medals. While biding time before returning home on a well-deserved leave to the planet of Flon D'Mar, he never imagines this function would prove to be the beginning of his worst nightmare.

The officer, having never been comfortable around politicians, realizes he needs to relieve himself after drinking too many spirits so he can tolerate this soirée. He decides to search for a more removed restroom after noticing these have become crowded. The soldier steals away from the main ballroom area to a side wing of the massive structure. As the din of the party fades away behind him, he admires the elegant fabrics draped down the sides of the walls lining this particular hallway. The path spills out to an empty atrium, exposing a waterfall that gently cascades down a rock wall with a constant but subtle splash into the pool of a grotto. Tosin sees a sign for bathrooms and heads toward another corridor. After proceeding down the deserted hallway, he hears two men talking. Something inside him—a gut feeling—causes him to pause before turning the corner. He hides behind one of the large granite pillars and eavesdrops on their conversation.

Faylen Clog is prime minister of the High Council, which governs the Rey-Lin system. The tall politician, with braids woven through a long mane of white hair overtop of a hardened face, hawkish nose, and a straight lip surrounded by a similarly bleached goatee and moustache, speaks to another council member. Deet

Tumarian, a frail-looking lawmaker with balding hair, and wire-rimmed spectacles laments in a mousey voice, "Dax is complaining that his contributions are too high. Stuttering as he continues, "He - he, he says it's becoming too difficult for him to make the payments."

"Nonsense … he's richer than half the system," scoffs the chancellor.

Deet continues, "I'm concerned there could be an audit if someone finds out. We could lose the next election … or worse!"

Faylen instructs, "Tomorrow, I want you to transfer all the *contributions* to a financial institution in the Aldo system, where I keep a secret account. I will give you the codes in the morning. And … I have a plan to *deal* with Dax. I have been speaking to Commander Duriness about executing an initiative. I call it … the *Daxian Resolve*. He now happens to have the crime lord's location and I explained that the High Council would like the System Guard's *assistance* apprehending him."

The diminutive politician nods in accordance as they start walking back to the party. Tosin rounds the corner of the hallway as they finish talking and nods politely at the senators before continuing on. He can feel them staring at him from behind, but he never looks back.

Clog questions, "Who was that?"

Senator Tumarian responds, "That is Major Tosin Luval."

"From the *Tal Rutette* offensive?"

"Correct," affirms Tumarian.

The prime minister orders, "Tell Duriness I want *him* to lead the campaign. It's perfect if something goes wrong."

"Blame it on the hero?" the small man adds, almost as a question.

"Exactly," Clog answers with a wry smile.

The following morning, Luval is packing for a shuttle back to his home planet of Flon D'Mar when his com bracelet—a device widely used for communication—starts to chirp. Tosin walks over to the dresser where the little metal band is resting and taps the top of it. "This is Major Luval."

A slightly distorted voice honks through the tiny speaker in the device. "Major Luval, you are ordered to report to Sulimay Command Central immediately. Guards will be at your hotel shortly to escort you to a waiting shuttle."

The officer hits mute on the small wrist piece, and sits down on the side of the bed. He contemplates before hitting the top of the small alloy wristband and replies, "Central, I think there's been a mistake. I am scheduled for leave. There has to be someone else."

The squawking voice returns, "Negative, your presence is mandatory by order of the High Council. Details will be forthcoming when you arrive at command."

Tosin spies the city's workings through the large window of his hotel room hundreds of meters in the sky. He misses the smell of the salt air and the simple life by the sea on his home world. In his mind, he vows, *This is the last one. I've got to get out.* After a moment, he taps the little device and confirms, "Copy all. Will update when I am airborne. Major Luval out."

After a brief suborbital hop in a government shuttle to the other side of Sulimay, the major peers out the window at a massive structure sitting by the edge of a vast ocean. The shuttle circles the facility then lands quickly. He and the two soldiers escorting him are peppered by a light rain, which reminds him of his home water world planet, as they walk briskly across the damp tarmac. Once inside, he is ushered into an expansive space filled with multiple large video displays painted on the walls like moving tapestries, and personnel transfixed to smaller monitors at their workstations. The soldiers guide Tosin into a side conference room and motion for him to be seated. After mutual salutes, the two escorts leave the room and shut the door. Luval has been trying to contact his wife all morning but can't seem to get through. He knows she will be waiting for him at Flon D'Mar's main spaceport and becomes concerned.

A heavyset man in a dark blue uniform with silver hair and his assistant, a younger woman with a yellowish complexion, narrow eyes, and straight black hair cut in a short bob, enter the room and sit down hurriedly. The assistant pulls out a small digital tablet, and her fingers begin to dance across the top of the translucent device.

Loland Duriness, joint commander of the System Guard, speaks in a baritone voice, "Major Luval, are you familiar with a man named Maytor Dax?"

Luval becomes agitated at the question due to its obvious answer and responds, "Dax is the most wanted crime lord in the solar system. Why am I here?"

"Our intelligence has exposed the Daxian Syndicate's central nest on Seltuvay's moon, Kree. We want you to lead an assault force to rid the system of this menace."

Tosin pauses for a moment and then says, "Why me?"

"The System Guard values your unique talents as a military tactician."

"Show me the intel."

The young woman slides the tablet across the table. The officer stops the thin transparent device before it falls off the table, then taps on it to view the video. What he sees is heartbreaking; women and children being beaten while they harvest leaves to make the narcotic Gelamine—a powerful and addictive drug.

The major, now interested in the operation, queries, "Troop strength? When do we leave?"

The commander details, "Ten ships, two platoons. You leave in three hours."

Alarmed, Luval protests, "*Three hours!* I need more time. They'll see us coming. We need a plan."

"You can do that on the way. You have complete control over the armada, but we need to act *now*. We suspect Dax has spies in the government, so the element of surprise is paramount. This is our best chance! Three hours!"

Commander Duriness and his assistant rise out of the chairs quickly, and a guard standing outside the door opens it for them. The man turns back toward Luval and with a stern face reminds him, "The High Council and the System Guard are counting on you, Major."

Tosin muses to himself, *Yeah, because Dax is getting tired of paying bribe money. Fine let's go get the bastard!*

Duriness salutes the major, who halfheartedly returns the gesture before the commander, with his assistant in tow, leaves the room. Tosin spies them through the window, now being followed by an entourage of soldiers, as they all depart the main control area. He quickly exits the conference room, moves to an open workstation, and starts to type. Images with numbers next to them appear on the monitors in front of him. After a moment, the face of his wife comes up on the display.

Desiree Luval's brown hair cascades down her neck and shoulders like a shimmering waterfall, reaching the small of her slender back. Her green eyes stare intensely at the major as deep red lips set in the sharp features of her face purse. She begins to speak in a surprised but soft tone. "Tosin? Where are you? You said eleven hundred. I waited at the spaceport, but an officer and three guards came and escorted me home. I asked what had happened, but they said it was classified and that you would call when you could. I'm worried. Are you okay?"

He assures her, "I'm fine, honey. They've ordered me on a miss—"

She interrupts, "Oh, *Tosin!* You said—"

"I know, I know. All I can say is … it *is* important, and I *will* be back tomorrow. *Promise.*"

"I'll have to tell Robey. You know your son misses you."

"Where is he?"

"Still at school. He's so excited to see you."

"Desiree, my love. *Tomorrow*. And I have something important to tell you. But I want to do it in person, so I'm waiting until I see you. I have to go. I love you. Bye."

The woman starts to reply, but he cuts the transmission with a tap on the keyboard and hurries out of central control. The same two guards who accompanied him earlier escort him out of the building, and into a waiting ground car before speeding off. After heading south for several kilometers, they arrive at the main gate of the System Guard's spaceport on Sulimay. One of the guards shows an ID at the fortified entrance, then the vehicle continues past the high dark gray *steelcrete* walls, deep into the center of the vast complex and onto an airstrip. The shape of a large military craft appears in the distance through the front windshield. Tosin leans back in his seat while the size of the craft grows larger. The charcoal gray exterior displays the familiar Rey-Lin logo on the twin tailfins—a triangle in the middle of two suns.

Ground crew with forklifts are busily stowing large cases in the underbelly of the ship. As they pull up next to it, the major exits the vehicle before it has completely stopped and walks over to a supervisor. He queries, "How long before we are fueled and packed?"

The soldier salutes and replies, "We'll be ready by the time you're on board, sir."

"I want extra *everything* for this mission. As much ordinance and supplies as the ship will handle."

"That will take more time, sir."

"How much?"

"Possibly a half hour."

"You have ten minutes."

"Roger, sir. Ten minutes. I will inform the ground crew."

The major continues on and enters the large vessel through an elevator tube under the center of the spacecraft.

Once the vessel is loaded, the ground crew all scurry away from the heavily armed ship. After a moment, thrusters roar to life like an angry monster, and it leaps powerfully off the concrete. It hovers briefly several hundred meters off the ground, then accelerates quickly before disappearing into the cloudy sky. The craft reaches orbit within minutes and takes its place in front of the other System Guard ships, already in formation, and awaiting Major Luval's arrival. The armada simultaneously fires their engines before collectively streaking out of orbit.

Tosin is typing on a glass portion of the armrest of his captain's chair. He stops, looks up, then calls to his executive officer, "Begin jamming the moon with long-range interference as soon as we're in range. Once we're within a hundred thousand, I want to split the ships up. The main complement with us, and two ships vectoring in on both zenith and nadir to the poles."

The executive officer, a young man with well-coifed blond hair, stationed at another console, acknowledges, "Copy, sir. Eight ships in formation, two on the poles." He issues the orders over their wireless, "Fleet, this is command. We are initiating long-range jamming procedures so communication will only be available at quantum level. One-Three-Eight and Two-Seven-Six, you will both veer off at one hundred thousand from Kree. One-Three-Eight will vector in at zero degrees toward the North Pole. Two-Seven-Six, you will slope in at a one-eighty in the direction of the South Pole. All ships acknowledge."

"One-Three-Eight copies."

"Two-Seven-Six rogers one-eighty vector to Kree South Pole."

The officer looks up from his console at Major Luval and confirms the orders have been received with a nod.

The rocky moon comes into view after an hour of flight. The devastation of the once lush world becomes apparent even from space. Deforestation and unchecked mining have left the celestial body a shell of its former self—and the charred section of Tal Rutette is a stark reminder of the last time he was here. The major looks over to his navigation officer and inquires, "Do we have any fresh recon video?"

The young man seated in front of a barrage of displays returns, "Negative, sir. Looks like they knocked out the drones that were deployed yesterday."

Tosin has a pensive scowl and thinks to himself, *They have to know we're coming.* He commands to the navigator, "Deploy two long-range probes *now.*"

The officer obeys. "I aye, sir, probes away!"

The sound of two large objects being jettisoned can be heard throughout the ship as they thunder away in blazes of light from the front of the craft. Tosin leans back in his seat and taps a small screen on the armrest, which shows a picture of his wife and son. He promises under his breath, *This is it, my love. My last mission!*

Major Luval requests an open channel from his communications officer. The soldier nods that he is live.

"This is Major Luval of the System Guard. We are here by order of the High Council to arrest Maytor Dax and his accomplices for crimes committed against the peaceful citizens of the Rey–Lin solar system. If you do not comply, we are authorized to use deadly force."

After a moment of silence, he asks, "Are you transmitting? Did they hear us? Tactical? What are you seeing?

His weapons officer shouts, "Missile lock! Major … they have a missile lock!"

"Evasive maneuvers. Fire all batteries!" As Tosin pushes a button on his command chair, the pilot stationed at a console in front and to the left of the major overrides the ship's automatic control and grasps a steering spire in the center of his console. The armada breaks formation, and veers away to avoid any incoming missiles. The military space cruisers, now in orbit, unleash a brutal bombardment on a section of the moon where the Daxian gang's hideout is suspected to be.

Several minutes into the attack, Major Luval notices that no missiles have been launched nor has there been any return fire from the surface.

"Cease firing! All stations stand down," he commands to the fleet.

The pulse cannons fall quiet. Shortly afterward, a signal comes through to the communication officer, "Sir. Kree is hailing us!"

"Well where were they ten minutes ago? Put 'em on," the major requests.

A baritone voice crackles through the speakers and reverberates around the control deck of the heavy star cruiser. "System Guard fleet commander, this is Quian Don, governor of Kree. Why have you fired at us! We received no warning from the High Council."

Tosin notifies the official, "Governor Don, we broadcast a request with a warrant for the arrest of Maytor Dax and his gang. If they did not want to comply, we were ordered to take them by force. Our sensors then picked up a missile lock from Dax's location, and we instituted defensive measures."

"Why didn't you inform us to take them into custody if you had a location!"

The major explains to the administrator, "Sir ... the High Council believes there is a mole and decided to execute this as a covert mission."

"Covert! You call blasting a town to kingdom come covert? We have teams moving into the area. There are a lot of casualties ..." The voice of the official seems painful as it trails off.

Tosin orders an expeditionary force down to the moon for inspection. The squad lands in two military shuttles at the blast site of the alleged missile lock—a small city on the southern hemisphere of the large moon. They deploy quickly after the ramps drop to the ground and commence a cleanup procedure. Moving through the rubble, they observe the carnage from the bombing.

The colonel leading the strike force radios back to the major, "Sir, I believe we have a ... situation down here."

Tosin responds, "Are you meeting resistance? Shall we send down more troops?"

The officer replies, "No, sir. There is … no resistance. But there are a lot of dead and wounded civilians down here. We have survivors claiming Dax and his men have been gone for a full day."

Major Luval bows his head in realization. *A setup. And I walked right into it!*

The major requests a channel to Duriness. "Commander. This is Major Luval. The target was compromised. Dax was tipped off. There are a lot of casualties, but they're all workers or slaves. The survivors said the gang fled yesterday."

The commander barks, "Didn't you check before you started killing people?"

Luval returns, "They faked a missile lock. We had no way of knowing."

Mortified, the commander chortles through the speaker, "This is going to be a diplomatic nightmare! The prime minister is going to need to speak to Quian Don. Recall the armada back to Seltuvay! But leave some troops to coordinate medical treatment and protection."

The major nods impatiently, waiting for the commander to finish before acknowledging, "Yes, sir. I have already spoken with him, and we are offering assistance now."

The commander concludes, "And, Luval? I want your ass in my office as *soon* as you land! Duriness out!"

While in flight back to the System Guard's main base on Seltuvay, he sits in his cabin trying to contact his wife with no success. He radios his communications officer, "Com! This is Major Luval. I need a line opened to my wife."

The officer squawks back, "I'm sorry, sir. Commander Duriness has ordered a blackout. We're dark until Seltuvay orbit."

Luval replies, "Copy. Thank you. Out."

He is snapped out of the flashback by the sound of the large metal door of his cell opening, revealing a guard holding a tray and shouting, "Wake up, Luval! Breakfast."

KANGAROO COURT

fter his debriefing and detention at System Guard Command on Seltuvay, Tosin begins the planetary journey to the High Council central complex in Solonos, the capital city of Sulimay. As Major Luval is sped away to the spaceport in a government shuttle, a man sitting next to him introduces himself, "Major Tosin Luval? My name is Adjunct Letony James II, and I am your lawyer.

Tosin responds, "No you're not. My lawyer is on Flon D'Mar. I need you to call Mr.—"

The man cuts him off. "I'm sorry, sir, but I have been *appointed* to you because this is a *military tribunal*, not a civil matter. That will inevitably come later." The aggravated officer begins to describe his suspicions when the attorney cuts him off. "Sir, I have gone through all of your testimony. We will present these issues in court however; I must caution you on implicating the High Council without definitive proof. It could have a … negative effect on your case." The major stares at him for a moment then bows and shakes his head in disgust.

Over the next several days, the ensuing uproar over what has now become known as the *Kree Massacre* is deafening and large protests are staged outside the walls of the government complex. Tosin must be hidden away in a deep part of the structure while the inquiry is being processed. He is finally granted a request to see his wife and child. Desiree and Robey are ushered into the small room. The main guard says, "I'm sorry, sir, but you only get five minutes. I have my orders."

The brown-haired woman hugs him tightly as Luval nods to the guard leaving the holding cell. He touches her fair skin and then says in an agitated whisper, "Desiree. This is a lie. I need … time to clear my name. It was … bad intel … I—"

She holds her finger up to his lips and speaks softly. "I know, dear. You could never do these things—"

He cuts her short, "No! I *did* do this! But they faked a missile lock! It was a ruse. They *knew* we were coming. I was set up! The High Council is corrupt, *and* there's a mole."

The slender woman sooths her loving husband by rubbing his shoulder then speaking softly in his ear. "Tosin, my love, you will be cleared."

He looks down at his son, who is trying hard not to cry. The boy looks very much like his father, and both of their green eyes meet as the soldier reassures his son, "Robey. My boy. You are only eight. But you must remember everything I've taught you and help your mother. You are the *man* of the house now. Understand?"

The boy looks up at his father and salutes. "Yes, sir! I will take care of Mom … sir!"

Tosin smiles and puts his hand on Robey's head. The guard reenters the room and taps the officer's shoulder. "Major, we have to go. I'm sorry, sir."

He hugs his wife, and then soldiers escort him out of the cell.

Faylen Clog and Deet Tumarian sit in a private office away from the main council chamber on an encrypted video call with Maytor Dax. The crime lord is enraged, and with his portly, beet-red face filling the screen, he begins screaming at the two politicians while bits of frothing effluvium exit his mouth. "Did you *really* think you could get rid of me that easily? I knew about this before that moron Luval did!"

Clog tries to calm the fat boss down by spinning the failure, "Dax, this was a setup. We didn't *want* to kill you. We needed a scapegoat. *We* tipped you off. I *know* who your moles are. This was all part of our plan."

Tumarian adds, "We knew you had another base."

Dax chortles, "This is gonna cost you … *big!*"

Clog shakes his head. "No … it's not. We *helped* you escape. Now you stay on your little … asteroid or wherever you are, and … you can keep your *business* going. We just want to keep the status quo. If not, the next force I send after you will *annihilate* the entire asteroid field you're in. I'm tired of you, Dax, and I really don't care what you threaten me with because *you* will go down long before I do. Furthermore, I will wipe everything and claim you're a delusional drug addict. Now treat this like a win and let's move on."

The obese criminal pouts on the screen momentarily, then waves his hand in the air. "Okay, okay. Ha ha, okay. But that's it, right?"

Faylen assures, "Yes, I've already spoken to the judge for the trial."

Deet Tumarian suggests, "We thought maybe you could help us … with a little collateral assistance."

Dax questions, "Oh?"

Faylen describes, "We think Major Luval will be more … cooperative if he knows his family's lives are at risk."

Tumarian informs, "We have the wife and child detained. Maybe they could … go missing?"

Maytor Dax smiles. "Ah … yes. Good idea. I can keep them with me for a nice long stay."

Tumarian adds, "The plan is to send him to Drotham."

Dax jumps. "Oh excellent! I have many associates there an—"

Clog interrupts, "Yes we know—many of them because of Major Luval. Warden Frukas has been informed of the situation. Once that's done, you can dispose of the wife and child."

Maytor Dax, grinning ear to ear, returns wryly, "My my, Clog, how you've changed."

The prime minister stares into the screen, his eyes now slits as the words leave his lips like bombs in the air. "This is it, Dax. I don't want anymore trouble from you."

Dax shouts, "We still need to talk about my pay—"

Clog hits the keyboard forcefully, ending the transmission, then trains a scowl at Tumarian, "Once this is finished, he has to go. I want security to keep an eye on all his contacts. Don't *do* anything. Just keep an eye on them."

"Yes, Mr. Prime Minister."

Faylen rises to his full height and leaves the room, slamming the door behind him.

The next day, after breakfast, a guard comes back and escorts Tosin from his holding cell deep in the center of the High Council complex to a chamber on the main floor to stand trial for the Kree Massacre. Seated next to his appointed advocate, Letony James II, the court bailiff requests that he stand. The major, now wearing his turquois and dark blue uniform adorned with medals, stands straight and looks forward seemingly into space as he listen's to the court officer.

"Major Tosin Luval, you are accused of war crimes against the citizens of Kree and the Rey-Lin system, including gross negligence, dereliction of duty, and murder. How do you plead?"

The soldier pauses for a long moment before answering. He stares directly at the judge and states, "Not guilty, Your Honor," before sitting down again.

The gallery of onlookers begins to murmur and scoff before the senior of three judges, by the name of Roder Orleg, a portly man with white hair, rounded face, and bright red cheeks, slams his gavel and commands, "There will be order during this proceeding! Anyone who causes disturbances in this courtroom will be jailed for *contempt*! In addition, if it continues, we will vacate the chamber and this trial will be held behind closed doors! Do I make myself clear!" He looks to his fellow jurists, who nod in agreement, then around the room, which is now deathly quiet, before continuing, "Let us begin with opening statements. Mr. Prosecutor, you may proceed."

Duran Duvay, the lead governmental attorney, reviews some notes on a tablet before standing to reveal a tall, thin body, smartly dressed in a dark gray suit and tie. The man with short, well-coifed, graying hair and a tanned complexion over sharp facial features begins to address the court, "Your Honors and distinguished citizens of Rey-Lin, we are gathered here today to adjudicate the terrible injustice done to the people of Kree. Major Tosin Luval, a decorated soldier, decided to take the law into his own hands and reign terror upon an unprotected city on a sovereign world. Let us begin with our first witness. The state calls Commander Leland Duriness to the stand."

The gallery turns and views as the commander enters the doors at the rear of the chamber. He proceeds slowly up the aisle with his assistant in tow, glaring angrily as he passes Luval before continuing to a podium at the right side of the judge's bench.

The prosecutor recites an oath. "Do you sir swear under the penalty of perjury that your testimony is truthful?"

The commander replies, "I do."

Duran continues, "Please state your name and title for the court."

"I am Leland Duriness, supreme commander of the System Guard of Rey-Lin."

"Commander Duriness, thank you for joining us here today. This is a matter of formality, but I must ask you, are you familiar with Major Luval?"

"I know all of my senior officers."

"Is he here today?"

"Yes."

"Can you point him out for us?"

The commander lifts his hand and points squarely at Tosin but does not look at him.

The prosecutor adds, "Thank you. Can you describe the events leading up to when he massacred those people?"

Letony stands, "Objection! Leading the witness."

Duvay redresses. "Let me rephrase. Can you describe the events leading up to the *incident* on Kree?"

"Yes, I can. We suspected that Maytor Dax had a central headquarters for his criminal empire on Kree. I was instructed by the High Council to deploy troops there for a reconnaissance mission and apprehension if possible. The deployment was to be led by Major Luval."

"Why did you need an *armada* to go to a small moon and arrest one man?"

"Mr. Prosecutor, have you ever served in the military?"

Judge Orleg intervenes, "Commander, please answer the question."

"Apologies, Your Honor. Maytor Dax has a vast criminal empire that employs hundreds, if not thousands, of mercenaries. We had no way of knowing what to expect."

"Why didn't you contact Governor Quian Don or the local guard detachment on Kree?"

"We had reason to believe there was a mole in our ranks, and that Dax has paid off members of the Kree ministry with bribes."

The gallery begins to murmur again, and Orleg warns, "One more outbreak and you're all gone!"

Duran pauses while the chattering subsides. "Did you give orders to indiscriminately *fire* on the planet?"

Duriness protests, "*No!* Absolutely not.*"*

"What happened after the assault?"

"I ordered the fleet back to our main base on Seltuvay."

"Anything else?"

"Once Major Luval was debriefed, no, Mr. Prosecutor. He was transferred here to Solonos and sequestered until this trial."

"Thank you, Commander Duriness. I have no more questions."

Judge Orleg directs, "Mr. James, your witness."

Letony James II advances to within a meter of the commander.

"Isn't it true that Major Luval told you that they believed they were being targeted with a missile lock from the surface?"

"He did mention it."

"So isn't standard procedure to retaliate?"

"There is nothing in the logs about a missile lock."

The advocate turns to face Tosin, who stares in disbelief before standing and blurting out, "That's a lie!"

Judge Orleg bellows, "Major! Sit down or you will be gagged and bound for the remainder of this hearing!"

Tosin complies, "Yes, Your Honors. I apologize," before taking his seat again.

The defense lawyer turns to the judges. "Your Honors, I request that a search be done by the IT department to ascertain why there is a discrepancy about these logs."

The judge turns to look at his two constituents and agrees, "Bailiff, please send a message to IT to do a sweep." The court officer obeys and begins typing on a tablet.

James surveys the commander for a moment then relinquishes, "I have no further questions."

The commander leaves the podium and exits the courtroom with his assistant following close behind. Judge Orleg consults with the other two jurists, before decreeing, "We will recess until after lunch," then slams his gavel down. The three judges are ushered out a side entrance as everyone rises to acknowledge their departure.

Tosin leans in to Letony's ear and whispers, "What the hell! Someone *erased* the files. You *have* to find those logs!"

"Major, I had no idea this happened. I went on your testimony. I should've made sure before the trial. I will do everything I can. I'm sorry."

The proceeding drags on after recess as both prosecutor and defender call witness after witness, including Quian Don, and display documents along with grotesque pictures showing the aftermath of the orbital bombing.

Major Luval is finally called to testify late in the afternoon. He recaps the events and asseverates his belief that he has been set up. The prosecutor states that without proof it will be difficult to corroborate his allegory. The judge then ordains, "I am adjourning this hearing until tomorrow morning so the information department can attempt to locate these *alleged* missing files." There is the familiar *clack* of his gavel, and all stand as the three judges file out.

Once the judiciary has left the courtroom, Tosin glares at the prosecutor before turning to his lawyer and whispering, "This is a witch hunt. When are you calling the crew from my ship to testify? They wi—"

Letony replies, "They swore under oath during their debriefings that it was a sensor malfunction. They're redeployed. Major, I warned you about involving the prime minister." The counselor informs his client, "I have received a message that your wife and child may be in mortal danger if you implicate the council."

Tosin yells in protest—a rare occurrence for him—startling some in the gallery, that are still filing out of the legal chamber, "This is a setup! I've been *framed!*

The advocate fears violence, and attempts to reason with the enraged officer. He counsels with a hushed voice, "Given the circumstances, maybe it's best if we plea bargain a charge of *negligence,*" James adds, "They mentioned you could be awarded a light sentence—possibly only house arrest due to your exemplary record with the System Guard. However, you will be dishonorably discharged and lose all your benefits." The lawyer beseeches, "For the sake of your family … and maybe my relatives as well, please consider the deal."

Tosin, realizing people are staring at him, quickly calms himself. After a pensive moment, he solicits the negotiator in a subdued tone, "Let's wait for IT. If they can't find the logs, we'll, deal." Then he seethes through clenched teeth, "But I don't care how long it takes,

I will get those bastards. Now … you *find* those logs. And get a security detail for my family."

Letony nods in accordance while looking down at a tablet. Luval waves at Desiree and Robey who are still in the back of the courtroom as soldiers arrive to take him away to his holding cell.

Tosin barely sleeps that night. His only comfort is the vision of his wife and child in their home by the sea on Flon D'Mar. He imagines staring out at the raging ocean with his nostrils full of the briny air above rocks being pummeled by waves of bluish-green water. He wonders if he'll ever see it or them again.

The following morning, Judge Orleg queries a technician, "Well?" The young man replies in a slightly trembling voice, "Your Honor, we were unable to retrieve the information due to what the specialists say is a data corruption. There is a backup, but that too is badly compromised and only shows information *after* the bombing. All the evidence points to what the crew members said … a sensor malfunction."

Tosin starts to shake his head and elbows his lawyer, who begins to request permission to approach the bench. The judge puts his hand up for the advocate to be silent, then bows his head momentarily before raising it, and staring directly at Tosin, "Will the defendant please stand."

Letony nods for him to obey Orleg's command. He stands, straightens his jacket, and turns toward the gallery behind him to view his wife and child sitting several rows back. He smiles at her before returning his gaze to the three jurists sitting behind the ornate wooden bench in front of him.

Judge Orleg decries, "Major Luval, after careful consideration of all the relevant facts, including consul with my other distinguished members here, it is this military tribunal's decision to make an example of you. The System Guard must be held to the highest standards of our laws. As such, we find you *guilty* of these horrific charges. If it weren't for your years of service, I would have you executed. Instead, you are hereby sentenced to life imprisonment on the penal colony moon of Drotham! Bailiff, remove the prisoner." He slams his gavel down to end the proceeding.

The disgraced officer stares in disbelief and realizes, not only was he framed; the trial was rigged as well. The patrons of the gallery are all cheering while Tosin's wife shrieks and crumbles in anguish over the verdict. The major glares back at the councilmen, who have been watching the trial from the back row, before several heavily armed guards usher him out a side door. His lawyer yells as he is led away, "I will start the appeals. We're not done, Major!"

Desiree and Robey are then also escorted out of the courtroom by another set of guards while she continues to sob uncontrollably. As Tosin walks down the hall to a holding cell, he can't stop replaying what James cautioned in his head once the kangaroo trial was over. *"Don't make trouble, do your time ... and your wife and son will be spared."* He has never felt so alone in his life.

Desiree Luval and her son, Robey, are waiting to be released from the High Council's complex after the trial. She looks down at her son and tries to comfort him, "Robey darling, this is all a misunderstanding. We will be going home soon."

Two men in dark clothing suddenly enter the room before one of them speaks in a forceful tone. "Ma'am, you and your son need to come with us ... now!"

The major's wife protests, "What is this? We—"

One of the men with black hair and glasses hits both the wife and child with a tranquilizer barb from a dart gun, and they crumble to the floor. The guard impersonators collect the two bodies in large black bags.

They spy the hallway in both directions before exiting the room and smuggling them out of the headquarters in a large rolling container.

PRISON PLANET

The voyage to the prison moon of Drotham around a gas giant named Lothi is long and uneventful. Lothi and Drotham are actually outside the Goldilocks Zone of the Rey-Lin star system. Drotham should be a cold, desolate rock, but the heat from Lothi's radiation has made the large moon a truly amazing world—complete with a breathable atmosphere, mountains, oceans, jungles, and deserts. But it is deadly. There are many wild animals on the moon, and as a penal colony, the wardens of both the men's *and* women's prisons find the horrific creatures an extra added bonus, ensuring there are no escapes from the prison planet. Tosin, unaware of his wife's abduction, sits, locked in chains, in the back of the space transport and plots a strategy to avenge himself. If he can win Drothamae, he can secure his freedom … *legally*. But he wonders; would they let him play?

Tosin had only been to Drotham twice before and both times were only layovers after escorting condemned souls to the planetary penitentiary. Upon his arrival he realizes this time will be different—a very lonely and dangerous place at best. Walking slowly off the space transport in his restraints and surrounded by six guards, the hangar has been emptied of all but essential personnel, who stare at him intently. He is escorted to a room, inspected by a doctor, then given a harsh disinfectant shower as if to wash off radiation even though he has none. The convicted soldier receives a red prison jumpsuit and is sent to a holding cell. After several hours of waiting, he hears the clacking of boots echoing off the concrete floor in the hallway, which eventually ceases in front of his cell. A series of beeps on the keypad outside disengages the lock of the large steel door, which swings open to reveal a guard with his helmet visor lowered. He points a pulse weapon at Tosin and barks, "Luval! Warden wants to see you. Try anything, and I vaporize you. Are we clear?"

The prisoner acknowledges, "Crystal."

He steps out of the small room, and they walk several hundred meters through a labyrinth of hallways to a lift, which ascends high into a tower. As the elevator opens, the prisoner views the lavish quarters with rustic wood furniture and paintings mounted along the walls. A man with short, cropped blond hair over an angular face and deep blue eyes sits at a desk finishing up a meal. He chews slowly, then wipes his mouth thoroughly before speaking, "Tosin Luval. Do you know who I am?"

The major smiles before answering, "Braytire Frukas, warden of the men's prison on Drotham."

"That's right, *prisoner* Luval. You have caused me a bit of a quandary, sir."

"Oh? Why is that?"

"Oh come now, Luval. There are at least fifty men here because of you. I've had to keep the place on a virtual lockdown ever since we received word of your conviction."

"Well, Warden, why don't you just give me a pulse weapon and I'll take care of that problem for you."

"Hah! And … there's a price on your head. It's gotten bad enough that I've had to brief all my men that I will have them summarily executed if I find out they killed you. In short … everyone here *hates* you."

"So let me go. This whole thing is a ruse anyway. I was framed. Prime Minister Clog is in bed with Dax. The whole system has become corrupt."

"Mmmm, well … that's not my business. I only want to keep law and order amongst the worst convicts in our solar system. Not an easy task, mind you."

"I'm sure it's not."

"No … it's not."

"So, ex-Major Luval, this brings me to my next question. How do you feel about participating in Drothamae?"

"I thought you'd never ask, Warden Frukas."

"Ah … well … this could work for both of us."

"Well it only works for me if I win … *Warden*."

"Yes, yes, of course, and participation is voluntary. We can't force anyone to play. But if you die, you're not my problem anymore."

Tosin focuses a steely gaze upon the warden. "I accept."

"Splendid. There's still a month before the next competition, so you will be kept in a special wing away from the other prisoners for your protection. You will have access to a private garden outside for an hour per day." The warden rises to shake Tosin's hand, but the soldier just stares at him until the warden lowers his arm.

"Guard! Take him away. One way or another, Luval, you will *not* be my problem for long."

Tosin smiles at him before the guards grab his arms and usher him out of the warden's lavish quarters.

Once he is alone, Braytire contacts Faylen Clog. The image of the prime minister appears on a screen mounted in the warden's desk.

"Warden Frukas, how are you today?"

"I am well, Prime Minister Clog."

"How is your new prisoner?"

"He has accepted the challenge of Drothamae."

"Excellent. Let us hope he doesn't win."

"It is a perilous game, Prime Minister. Anything can happen. I will contact you just before the game begins. I have some … *arrangements* to tend to."

"Understood. Clog … out."

The screen goes black, and the warden leans back in his chair and thinks for a moment before leaning toward the desk and typing in some commands on a keyboard. Several images of prisoners come up on the screen as he reviews contestants for the upcoming challenge.

Several weeks into his internment, Tosin views the image of Letony James II on a screen from one of a row of terminals setup for prisoners to communicate off world.

The prisoner is agitated about his family as he speaks to the lawyer. "I can't get through to my wife. What's going on?"

The lawyer replies, "Mister Lu—"

"*Major* Luval!"

"Yes, M-Major Luval. There was … an incident after you were taken away. We believe your wife and son were kidnapped."

"*Kidnapped!* And you're only telling me about this now? You *assured* me they would be safe!"

"Yes, sir, I know. And the System Guard is searching for them now. They are very upset about this."

"*They're* upset?"

"Major. Please. I have filed the paperwork for your appeal and found a specialist in data retrieval. He thinks he can rebuild the data from the corrupted file. But I hear you have accepted the challenge of Drothamae. Maybe you should wait before doing something so drastic."

"I will need to talk to the warden."

"Be careful. I will contact you when I know more."

The screen goes dark, and Tosin turns toward one of the guards. "I need to see the warden … *now.*"

Luval waited a day before Frukas would see him again. The jailer-in-chief makes a rare journey down from his tower through a large enclosure with multi-levels of cells to a disserted hallway where prisoners in solitary confinement are located. A guard punches a code on the keypad and a large metal door swings open. Frukas stares at the major, who is lying on his cot, then speaks, "Well, what do you want?"

"Warden, are you familiar with my case," questions the prisoner.

The blond-headed man chuckles before responding, "Huh-huh-huh. *Familiar?*" You're the biggest pariah in the system."

"Where are my wife and child?"

"How should I know?"

"I have an appeal coming. I've decided to hold off on competing until after my appeal … and they find my family."

"First off … *prisoner* Luval. Typically, once a player has accepted the challenge of Drothamae, he is bound by his word. Second … if … and I mean *if* I knew where your wife and child were, it would be best for them if you played the game.

"So you're in on it too."

"I don't know what you're talking about. I am merely stating that if someone has gone to the trouble of abducting them, there must be a reason. Has anyone contacted you?"

"Only my joke of a lawyer."

"No one else?"

"How the hell can anyone contact me? I've been in solitary for weeks."

"I will make some calls to see what is happening with the investigation … as long as you honor your agreement to compete. Deal?"

"Deal."

As the warden leaves his cell he adds, "And drop the appeal until *after* the competition. No distractions before the game." Luval nods before the guard slams the door shut.

The final weeks leading up to the contest have been tedious. Trying to sleep in solitary confinement has been even more difficult. The disgraced soldier is anxious the night before the match; however, he finally calms himself by recalling a better time and the sight of his wife as he falls asleep and dreams.

Tosin has just returned from a particularly difficult mission to their home by the sea on Flon D'Mar. After Desiree makes his first home-cooked meal in several weeks, they retire early. He is shaken awake in the middle of the night by a bad dream. A light breeze wisps through the open windows on the unusually warm evening and cools the bedroom. He runs his fingers through his wife's flowing brown hair and listens as she breathes softly. She awakens and turns to face him. They quietly gaze sideways at each other before she whispers softly, "I'm so happy your home. How long do you have?"

The soldier puts a finger up to her lips to stop her from talking. "I'm here now, my love. I don't want to think about anything else but you."

They embrace tightly as their lips meet for a long and sensual kiss. She pulls away slightly and smiles at him, then slides her body slowly over on top of him. Their passion stretches on deep into the night until, soaking wet, they finally fall asleep from exhaustion.

*"D*o your time. Don't make trouble. And your wife and child will be spared."

The words echo over and over again, swallowing his peaceful dream before he is awoken by the sound of a guard screaming at him.

"Luval!"

Tosin, startled by the man's yelling, sits up in the bed quickly. "What the hell?"

"I've been trying to get you up for five minutes. You were talking in your sleep. It's time. You ready?"

"I need ten minutes, a shower, and some food."

The guard orders, "Here's your flight suit. Put it on or I'll shoot you now."

The prisoner pulls down his drawers, sits on the toilet, and relieves himself while staring at the guard.

Once finished, he begins to dress and inquires, "Don't I get a meal?"

"All the contestants ate. You overslept."

"I'm in solitary," complains the prisoner.

"Hurry up! They're all waiting to get a look at you."

"Why are they so excited?"

"Are you kidding? A chance to take down a guardsman? We've had to keep most of the prison on lockdown since you got here."

"Should be over soon."

"The whole place will sleep better once you're dead."

"Or free," comments Tosin under his breath as he laces up his boots.

"You're a disgrace to the System Guard. Shut up and let's go."

The guard steps back from the door with his hand firmly on his weapon as Tosin zips up his gray flight suit and walks past him slowly. They continue down the hallway and into another section of the prison with multiple floors of cells lined on each side of an open atrium. As he is escorted past the prisoners, they begin banging on their doors and taunting him.

"You're dead, Luval!"

"You'll never make it past the first checkpoint!"

Tosin spies a wide grin from underneath the guard's tinted visor as the jailer chastises him, "Odds are pretty high you won't make it very far."

Tosin replies curtly, "I'm not a betting man."

The two stop at the end of the corridor, and the guard keys in a code on a device on his left arm, allowing the large metal door to open out into the main courtyard. Tosin pulls a set of sunglasses out of his top pocket—one of only two things he was able to keep once he got to prison— and puts them on to shield his eyes from the glare of the moon's gas giant—Lothi. He surveys the shuttles parked by a row of hangars a hundred meters away. Mechanics and technicians are busily hurrying around the vehicles preparing them. Several are stowing missiles and weapons into the large, angular, charcoal-gray machines while others retract fueling hoses from ports on the stubby wings of the menacing-looking transports. Braytire Frukas, now wearing his military dress uniform with gold bands on his sleeves and hat, orders all the contestants to line up. Once everyone is quiet, he begins to bark.

"All right, listen up. Most of you know the rules, but as warden of this prison facility, I am obligated by law to repeat them to you out loud. One: you have twenty-six hours to get the Drothamae into the nulling ring before it explodes. Two: a referee ship will destroy any ship that tries to escape. Three: the referee will also destroy anyone who shoots at a vehicle not carrying the Drothamae, or a referee ship. Four: you must pass a checkpoint to receive coordinates for the next one. Five: any deaths amongst the crew of any shuttle will deem that team disqualified, and, as you may have surmised, the referee will blow your ship up. Six: if the Drothamae is destroyed before it is placed in the nulling ring, a new one will be deployed, but the clock will not be reset. Weapons and shields will become operational at the start of the game and will be disengaged at the finish. All inmates must exit their vehicles at the end of the contest, or the vehicle and any occupants will be destroyed. Okay, men, you were given your ship assignments last night. Lets play *Death Ball!*

A cheer roars up from the men as they scramble toward the vessels. Tosin spots a ship with a large number two painted in white on the sides of the vehicle and sprints to it. None of the contestants know who is with whom, but they all have keycards with a number on it that will only work on their assigned ships. As he leaps up the ramp at the back of the vehicle, he spies a large, bald man approaching him. This is his worst nightmare. The man's name is Cholash, a notorious murderer who he wounded and captured several years ago. He races onto the vehicle and braces himself against the bulkhead as the grotesque man runs up into the rear of the ship. The ogre grumbles as he limps, out of breath, at the top of the ramp. "Luval, where are y—"

Tosin swings a metal pipe onto his head and drops him. As he lays unconscious, Tosin checks his vitals to make sure he's still alive and then secures him in a seat in the rear of the shuttle. Two more prisoners stop at the top of ramp and look surprised at the sight of the large man bound and gagged. Tosin queries, "Are we gonna have any problems?"

The smaller of the two answers first, "Whoa, not me. I wanna get off this rock! Name's Tiller. Yukev Tiller."

The thin, lanky man with a pasty complexion, tuft of red hair, and childish face smiles as he offers his hand. Tosin lowers the pipe and shakes it quickly, then trains a stare at the other man. The dark-skinned prisoner holds up his hands and returns, "No problem here, boss. Dey calls me Zander."

"Okay then, let's get to work."

Tiller questions, "What about Cholash? If they find out, we c—"

Tosin cuts him off, "They won't. We'll deal with him later. We need to get in the air."

Zander adds, "I's good wit duh weapons."

Tosin inquires, "You know what you're doing?"

Zander beams a smile, and his teeth seem extra white contrasted by his dark brown skin as he replies, "Better wit a pot n' spatula but holds my own."

Tosin dashes forward and climbs a ladder onto the flight deck, surveying the cockpit—two identical stations next to each other with a center console between them are populated with a dizzying array of switches and screens. The only difference between them is a retractable steering yoke on the right-side navigation post. The experienced pilot begins prepping for takeoff as Tiller comes up the ladder and hops into the co-pilot's chair before declaring, "Guess I've got shotgun!"

Tosin turns with a scowl and questions, "Do you know how to navigate?"

Tiller gives a thumbs-up sign as he begins working the controls.

As the engines power up, the major cautions, "Don't send us into a mountain!"

He pulls back hard on the yoke, and the craft lurches up off tarmac, then gains altitude quickly. Yukev pushes some switches, and the holographic image of a topographical three-dimensional map of the moon is displayed between them, with other numbers visible across the front windshield. He and the pilot observe the other ships assembling in a formation as they jockey around each other for position. A bright red craft is in the lead, and a voice comes over the loudspeaker and headphones.

"This is the referee. Line your ships up and circle the area displayed on your maps at an altitude of five hundred meters. Do not exceed two hundred kilometers per hour or you will be penalized. The Drothamae will be deployed shortly."

Tiller shakes his head and comments, "Penalized, meaning they'll blow us out of the sky!"

Tosin turns his head, now with a special visor down across his eyes, and commands, "Cut the chatter. Don't talk unless you have to. Use hand signs. We don't want to let anyone know what we're doing because all communication is being monitored. Got it?"

Yukev smiles and gives another thumbs-up sign. Zander is down in the cargo bay strapped in at a weapons station. He checks a screen to confirm that all of the weapons systems are online. Tosin cautions the gunner through the on-ship com system to his headphones, "Zander, conserve ammo! Don't shoot anything without asking me first. Okay?"

Zander replies, "Got it, boss. But what you gonna do 'bout a grappler wit dat big man out?"

Tosin answers, "Don't worry about that moron. He's useless. I rerouted grappler controls up here. We'll do it ourselves. He's a homicidal maniac, and he'd rather die murdering me than try to win. He'll get us all killed. Let me know if he wakes up, and I'll put him out again. As long as they see his vitals, we're fine."

"Okay den. You da boss, man."

A big metallic ball starts to hover up into the air, and a large chronometer with bright red numbers in the middle of the cockpit begins to count down. The timer decrements to zero, and a buzzer sounds. The LED clock resets to twenty-six hours and begins to count backward again. Tosin muses to himself, *Game on!*

Suddenly there is a crash as one of the ships slams into the side of their vehicle. Another ship to the right starts to tack sideways toward them, and Tiller lets out a shriek. Tosin pushes the yoke forward, and the shuttle creaks and moans as it dives and foils the pincer move by the attackers. The second ship can't compensate and smashes into the craft that initially hit them. Both explode in a massive fireball as Tosin veers to avoid the falling debris.

Tiller shakes his head and barks, "So it's gonna be like this then? Well that's number three and nine outta the way."

Tosin has a smirk and answers under his breath, "Yep. Two down. Seven more to go."

The number five ship grabbed the Drothamae whilst Tosin avoided being destroyed by the first two ships, and sped away in an easterly direction. Defense is just as important as offense in this contest. There were many places to hide on this deadly moon. A popular trick is to *grab and hold* until new coordinates are broadcasted to the contestants. While the ships all have regular radar and navigational equipment, only the referee knows where all the individual craft and the Drothamae are.

Shortly after the craft with the ball speeds off, another with the number seven on the side of it starts to pursue Tosin, and again he needs to demonstrate his piloting propensity as his adversary attempts to pounce on him.

Yukev remarks, "Hey you think there's a bounty on you? Because these bastards don't seem to care much about going after the ball."

"Yeah … um, I probably wasn't the best teammate to be stuck with for this," replies Tosin. "Zander! Keep the shields up because I don't think the rules apply to us anymore!" The craft trains its guns on them and opens up with a hail of laser fire.

The navigator shouts, "So what, we're just supposed to take this without returning fire?"

The pilot demands, "Do *not* return fire. That's exactly what they're hoping for. Lemme handle this." He then pushes on the yoke and puts their craft into a vertical dive. Tiller yells above the whine of the engines, "I'm glad I didn't eat that much this morning because looks like it's gonna get hairy!"

After a moment, the skilled aviator pulls back hard on the stick, levels the ship only meters from the ground, and points it at a sierra in the distance. The other craft follows close behind, and Tosin realizes that the pursuing ship also has an excellent pilot. He muses to himself, *Hmmm, this isn't going to be easy.*

As they reach the elevations, he enters into a deep ravine at breakneck speed and follows a river with cliffs on either side, only meters from the ship's stubby wings. Tiller blurts out, "What the hell are you doing!"

"Didn't you ever play video games?"

"Yeah, but I lost most of the time!"

"Well, I always got a perfect score," claims Tosin as the airframe moans in complaint at how it is being flown."

The assailing ship can't compensate for the sharp turn Tosin has just made and slams into the rock wall, letting off a large explosion from the onboard munitions it is carrying. The crew collectively lets out a holler. Zander turns back toward the cargo hold and notices that Cholash, with a dried blood streak down the side of his head, has awakened and is trying to break free of his restraints. The gunner contacts Tosin, and the pilot spies a clearing by the side of the river. He sets their craft down hard, quickly undoes his harness, and leaps down the ladder of the flight deck. He sprints into the hold where the large man has successfully managed to get one of his arms free of the restraint.

In one seemingly fluid motion, the guardsman grabs a metal rod from the side of the bulkhead and leaps the final three meters at the murderous convict, bringing the pipe squarely down on Cholash's head, thus knocking him out again. He turns to Zander and commands, "Tie him up again. And make sure to double up the restraints. If he gets loose, we're all in danger."

Zander nods in agreement. The pilot surveys the second stream of blood coming down the large man's head and turns to Yukev and Zander. "Any of you have any medical training?

Zander grins. "I ain't no doctor, but I done patched up some fellas befoh."

"Okay, clean him up and dress those wounds. We have to keep him alive." He turns to the navigator. "Tiller, are the shields still up?"

"Yeah."

"Keep it that way. I got a bad feel—"

Just then, a ship with a number six on the side drops down in front of them and starts firing. Tosin leaps up the ladder back into the pilot chair and heaves the ship back into the air to avoid the laser blasts. He shouts, "We've been tagged!

Tosin pushes the craft straight up out of the ravine and banks hard sideways. He complains to the navigator, who is struggling to get back in his seat and secure his harness, "We need a place to hide and find that damn tracking device or we're going to be *dead!*"

Tiller warns, "The shields won't take too much more of this. You better do something *now!*"

The pilot steels himself and comments under his breath, "Okay I've had enough of this guy." He points the grappling gun at the pursuing craft, centering the crosshairs of the targeting computer on its front windshield, and unleashes the harpoon full force. The grapple smashes through the front window of the ship, killing the pilot and navigator immediately. He retracts the cable and pulls hard on the yoke, sending their craft upward. The number six ship is now caught in a flat spin, and falls out of the sky onto a grassy meadow below, igniting in a fireball. Tosin smiles and says, "Oops, I guess I hit the wrong button." The other two members of the crew both start to laugh.

Yukev comments, "Wow, no law against that one because we're still here, huh?"

Tosin turns to Yukev. "Find us a spot in a cave somewhere. We need to shield the ship and figure out where the hell that bug is."

The navigator nods and begins to type in some commands on the keyboard. The holographic map between them updates, and he points at a location.

"Verness Caves. They should do."

The pilot agrees and begins a long turn. A broadcast on the computer informs them that new coordinates have been issued. The numbers are painted translucently on the windshield. Tosin comments, "Hopefully, they'll go after the ball instead of us."

Tiller adds, "Yeah, and we can find that bug.

THE ENEMY OF MY ENEMY

T he High Counsel chamber features an elevated ceiling supported by stone columns, etched with ornate designs. The walls of the room are adorned with tapestries hanging down from the ceiling. Faylen Clog's hardened face, looking as if it was carved out of pure rock, watches the game intently on his screen. He and Tumarian are presently the only ones in the chamber. The prime minister speaks with an almost hypnotic tone under his breath. The words seethe from his mouth like verbal serpents winding their way to his listener's ears, "Councilman Lieth will have to be dealt with if we are to consolidate power. He is a progressive, and we must move quickly to execute our plan—*complete* control under the guise of conservative reform."

Deet Tumarain replies, "Yes, but … what you suggest … is treason. I am not sure that I am comfortable with this course of action."

Clog becomes irritated and scowls at the diminutive man before raising his voice. "It isn't treason if no one knows of the plan. Your complicity puts you at risk as well. Best you hold your tongue or lose it."

The smaller man wilts into the high-backed chair as Clog's words echo through the granite chamber, then fade away.

"Dax has men on Drotham," reminds the prime minister.

Tumarian responds, "Well we have the warden as well, sir."

Maytor Dax is a despicable being. The son of a clone, he is an anomaly that should not have happened. Born despite pregnancy blockers, the short, obese humanoid with different color eyes offset on a warted face is truly difficult to look at. However this genetic abomination was born with a mutation: possessing the ability to regenerate most of his decrepit body. Short of removing his head, he is almost impossible to kill.

Dax realized at an early age he had a knack for all things sinister or illegal. After being a low-level lieutenant in a notorious gang, he found an opportunity to dispatch their leader, then by consolidating many of the other gangs with brute force, he created the most feared criminal empire in the system. The Daxian Cartel now holds a monopoly on drugs, gambling, prostitution, and smuggling. With deep pockets from dark profit, he has bribed or blackmailed members of the High Council and their families. Everyone despises this monster, but no one can, or would move against him without committing political or, worse, mortal suicide.

The council agreed to mount the Daxian Resolve campaign. It seemed easy. They knew where he was. Send the System Guard to his fortress on a moon named Kree orbiting the planet Seltuvay, the third planet in their system, and just wipe him out. The guard had unlimited firepower, and it should have been like shooting fish in a barrel. But with numerous spies inserted in the government, no matter how secretive they tried to be, he always stayed one step ahead. Two days before the campaign was set to begin, and long before Major Luval knew about it, Dax began covertly removing all of his personnel and operations off the moon to a secret location on a rocky asteroid in the *Gureeg Asteroid Belt* at the edge of the solar system. The evil overlord abandoned his crime headquarters, leaving behind only people who owed him money and slaves. He promised to erase their debt, and give them freedom, as long as they didn't talk or flee the moon—only to become casualties in a ruse that became the *Kree Massacre.*

The remote asteroid complex is not as posh as his headquarters on Kree. But the hideout is well stocked and heavily armed. Dax even outfitted the planetoid with deep space sensors and radar-jamming equipment. The rotund thug, with patches of straw-like hair around his bald scalp, watches the game on a large video screen mounted on the wall of an underground office. Maytor furiously chews on a large chunk of meat and yells at the screen, "Mmmm ugh. You're *dead*, Luval! Heh heh heh," as pieces of food fall from his mouth onto the floor.

The number two ship makes the five-hundred-kilometer run over the Erness Meadows in good time even though it is in need of repair. Tosin can sense that the airframe and engines are starting to feel the fatigue from the pounding the craft has taken. He expertly drops the ship into a crevice that leads into a dark cave. Yukev turns on the exterior floodlights, and water cascading down the dark rock walls reflects the beams, illuminating the entire chamber. Tosin gently lands the vessel, and the engine's whine begins to pitch down as he shuts the craft off. The pilot opens the back cargo ramp, and they walk to the rear of the ship. He casts a glance at Cholash, who has regained consciousness. Tosin has the pipe in his hand and warns the large man, "We're completely shielded down here. One move and I will end you. What do you know?"

The murderer shakes his head from side to side and speaks in a gruff voice, "Not much. Kill you. Go free. All other ships in on it. Warden in on it. Everyone in on it."

Tosin turns and trains the pipe at Zander and Yukev. "This true?"

The navigator puts his hands up. "We never thought you'd make it into the air!" He points at Cholash and continues, "He was supposed to take you out at the starting line. After you dropped him, we just decided to play along. At that point, we figured they were gonna kill us too. So we decided our best bet was to help you. Now we're all dead men."

Tosin sneers, "Where's the bug?"

Yukev replies, "We don't know. The tech crew must've installed it during their prep. I swear, I really don't know!"

The guardsman stares at Zander, who adds, "Easy, boss. He's tellin' duh truf. Duh orders got told tuh us by duh guards last night while we was in our cells. You's neveh s'ppose ta get dis fah. You was dead man walking since you done got heh."

"Well, you failed. I'm still here, and I should leave you all in this cave to rot," seethes the pilot.

Yukev interrupts, "You can't do this alone. Plus, we're *living* proof! We can still help you. We can still win this!"

Tosin yells as he slams the pipe against the side of the vehicle, "Where's the damn tracking device!"

Cholash discloses, "Think know where. Saw men working. But buried deep in ship. Not easy to find."

Yukev blurts, "Wait a minute! I can use our nav system to find it. I just need to reprogram some code."

"So lemme guess, you know tech too?"

"Oh yeah!" The slight man boasts loudly, "I was one of the main hackers of the government mainframe last year. That's why I'm here. I'll be in there in a couple of minutes!"

"What else can you do?" queries the pilot.

"Well, I think I can modify our nav system so we know where everyone—and the ball—is."

"Suicide switch?"

"That one's a little tougher, but I'll try."

Tosin looks around at the three men before speaking. "All right look. You know who I am. You probably know I was railroaded. But that's the past. Honestly, I doubt they were ever going to let you live since you knew they wanted to kill me. I know a lot of the System Guard's tricks. They changed the codes, so I can't help you there. But I can keep you alive. If we make it out of this, you really do have a shot at freedom. But it's going take teamwork. So … what do you say?"

The three convicts look at each other, then nod in agreement. Tosin adds, "Okay, cut Cholash loose." He warns the big man, "You try anything, I drop you again. Understand?"

The large man nods. "Me understand."

Zander undoes the restraints, and Cholash unleashes a right fist squarely on Tosin's jaw, summoning a spurt of blood from the guardsman's mouth.

The other two jump back as Cholash chuckles. "Now even." He rubs his own head.

Tosin wipes the blood from his mouth, and all are quiet until he grins and starts to laugh. He puts out his hand and agrees, "Okay fair enough. But we have to work fast!"

Their laughs echo off the chamber walls. Tosin then barks a couple of orders. "Zander, check all our munitions. Do you have any mech skills?"

Zander replies, "I can shoot good, but I's better at cookin' den fixin'."

Yukev shouts down from the flight deck into the cargo hold as warning claxons start to sound, "You might want to get outta here for a minute or two!"

All three ask in unison, "Why?"

Yukev returns, "I'm trying to disengage the suicide switch, and the ship ain't happy. There's a chance it'll blow up!"

The other crewmembers get out of the ship by scrambling down the ramp, then sprint for safety behind some rocks at the far edge of the cave. They wait tensely for several minutes before the sirens go quiet. Yukev saunters down the ramp and boasts, "Got it! Who's better than me, huh?" Just then, a loose section of the bulkhead falls and smacks him in head. The three men walk back over and begin to laugh as Yukev pushes the piece out of the way and rubs his head.

Maytor Dax is sitting in front of several screens, reviewing information while making rude sounds as he gorges himself with the leg of an animal. There are bits of food all over the desk and floor as he shoves the meat into his slightly disfigured mouth. A servant enters the room to request if he needs anything. "Excuse me, Your Excellency, but shall I bring you anything else?"

Effluvium ejects out of the fat man's mouth as he yells, "Wine! I need more wine, you imbecile! And get Rathen's ass in here now!"

"Yes, Your Excellency. Right away."

A short man with white curly hair, pasty skin, bifocal glasses and drooping cheeks shuffles into the room and stands in front of the desk while the grotesque man continues to fill his mouth with food. The aide inquires cautiously, "Yes, Your Excellency. What may I do for you?"

Dax retorts, "Rathen, have you seen this mess? I paid a fortune! All they needed to do was kill that bastard before the game started, and it would've been all over! Now I have the Council breathing down my neck! Get me the warden on Drotham … now!"

The albino man with pink eyes distresses as he replies, "Your Excellency, with respect, may I remind you there is a mandatory blackout during the game. I do not believe we can contact him until it is over."

Maytor is silent and brooding for a moment. Suddenly, he turns the entire desk over sending screens, food and wine everywhere as he jumps up from his chair. He pulls a weapon from his side and trains it on the frail man before speaking in a low gravely tone. "I don't care how you do it, but you get a message to my men on Drotham to find Luval and *kill* him. And get Braytire Frukas on the line in ten minutes or you are a *dead*! Understand?" Maytor fires several blasts above Rathen's head, and pieces of the ceiling fall as the waif runs for his life out of the room. Dax then demands, "Get someone in here to clean this mess up." He fires another round at the wall, blasting a hole in it before adding, "And get me more wine, damn it!"

Warden Frukas sits in a citadel high atop the main extension of the compound dining on fresh delicacies brought to him from the water world Flon D'Mar— which is responsible for much of the seafood consumed in this solar system. His high brow creases and his lips are pursed with concern as he chews slowly watching the screen with uneasiness. After the loss of the number six ship, the warden debates—for the first time in its history—whether to call off the game. The consequences of following the prime minister's orders to assassinate Tosin Luval weigh heavily on the jailer's mind. The whole thing stinks, and he isn't in the mood to continue getting his hands dirty. The prison had been a model of law and honesty until Clog's administration came to power.

Now he finds himself essentially in bed with the same wretched man the government is trying to dispatch. There has to be a way out of this. He needs to think. Suddenly his communication device starts to beep. Frukas is curious because all external lines are shut down during the game due to security precautions. He wonders how this transmission managed to get past the firewalls? He pushes a button on the side of his desk, and a fuzzy figure appears on the screen. "Braytire! Is that you? This connection is crap! I paid a fortune for the death of this son of a bitch! I didn't even care about this guy. This was Clog's request. Surely with a prison full of murderers, you should be able to kill one damn bastard … right?"

The warden, surprised by the call, disavows, "I don't know what you're talking about. How did you even get this number? Do you know who you are speaking with?"

"Don't you give me *that*! I know *exactly* who I'm talking to? Your boss *ordered* you to have Tosin Luval assassinated. Here's the deal. Either you kill him, or I kill your entire family on Seltuvay. Don't try to warn them. My men are already there. He dies … or they die. Dax, *out!*"

Braytire sinks back into his chair, wipes his mouth with a napkin, then leans forward and summons his guards. They sprint in, and he barks, "Where the hell is he?"

One of them answers, "Who?"

"You know who—Luval! Where is the number two ship!"

"We don't know exactly, Warden. We lost track of them near the Verness Caves."

The warden snaps, "Idiots! Then they're *in* the caves! It's shielding their tracking device. Dispatch a squadron and destroy them!

A guard cautions, "But, sir, we have no legal reason—"

The warden shouts, "Reason? They're off track, and as far as I'm concerned, they are trying to escape. Kill them now or I will have you shot for insubordination!"

The guards answer in unison, "Yes, sir!" as they spin on their heels and hurry out of his office.

THE APPLE FELL FAR

Yukev wipes his brow and complains to the pilot, "They did a number with those laser blasts to the starboard engine. I'm not gonna be able to give you full power without some spare parts."

Tosin inquires, "And if I could get them?"

"Uh, not sure what you're thinking, but even if I got them, it would take some time. Time we ain't got," pointing at his com bracelet, "Know what I'm saying?" He adds, "We don't even know where the ball is."

The pilot speaks under his breath. "It's not for the game. We're going to need a quick getaway with full power. Doesn't matter if we win now. We're marked. We all know too much."

"Get me the parts, and I'll give you orbital capability. I got a trick for these engines … ha ha ha."

"What about the bug?"

"Found that first. Turns out it wasn't as deep as Cholash thought." He holds up the little device.

Tosin grabs it out of Yukev's hand, throws it on the floor, and stomps it with his boot, smashing it to pieces. "Are you sure there aren't any more of them?"

Cholash, who is sitting several meters away, wrapping his head wound, interrupts, "No time. Heard mechs complain they wanted backup but game starting. Only one."

Tosin faces Yukev. "Okay then, how long?"

The thin man projects, "Maybe ten or fifteen. Just got one more thing to do."

As he runs up the ramp of the ship and starts to work, he remembers his past.

Yukev's family isn't even from Rey-Lin. No one is. It was colonized several thousand years ago by humanoids from another system. All of the original inhabitants come from somewhere else. Tiller's family migrated here due to persecution of their religion. Worship of deities, monotheistic or otherwise, became forbidden on their planet, so Yukev's forefathers made the long journey almost a century ago. While their ships used light-speed travel, the journey took many years, and by the time they arrived in this system, *Quantum Matter Shifting* had been discovered.

It didn't matter though, because to a religious sect, the thought of having yourself; dissected by lasers, stored as a digital file, beamed to a pool of biomass slime on the other side of a galaxy, reconstructed, and then zapped with a high-energy pulse to come back to life, was heresy. Their argument being the soul only lives in the original version and it is essentially suicide to kill one's self in order to be transported. Hence the *faithful* would rather putter through space for eons on a vehicle the size of a city rather than use such a demonic device.

Yukev didn't much care much for his family's religious ways and rebelled against his parents' strict upbringing at an early age. The boy never understood why a deity would need to have its subjects pray to it constantly. If it was that vain, it wasn't anyone he cared to worship. The boy was academically brilliant. He had been tested when he was younger, and his aptitude for mathematics, science, and technology was extremely high. He graduated high school at the tender age of eleven and was accepted to the illustrious Science Academy on Sulimay with a full scholarship. Much to his disappointment, the Tiller family thought it was unnatural and believed he should wait until he was older. His father also insisted he learn their farming business. Yukev grew to hate livestock. The smell of it, the taste of it, the very sight of an animal affected him greatly. Not because he hated wildlife, he just didn't want to kill it. He became a vegan at an early age and told his parents the he could no longer eat *anything with a face.*

A year later after his twelfth birthday, and despite the strong objections of his father, he secured passage on a *Star Liner* with money he had saved up and headed off to Sulimay to study at the academy.

His first few years were sublime and uneventful. But the perils of growing into a teenager took their toll on him. First came the fact that his coding skills on a computer were far superior to even his professors. His innate ability to understand even the most complex problems put him into a league of his own. He became withdrawn due to the difficulty of socializing with people who didn't understand his intelligence. Yukev couldn't even talk about the weather without attempting to explain complicated computer modeling that predicted when it would rain and why. Consequently, all of his *alone time* led to hacking anything with a processor.

And then there was … a girl. While not the prettiest female at school, she was extremely intelligent, and they would talk for hours about complex algorithms. For a moment, life was grand. But then came the scandals. The girl had become pregnant, and common perception was that Yukev was the father. Though they had never been intimate, she had implicated him because she couldn't divulge her secret relationship with the son of a member of the High Council. Yukev was ostracized and expelled from the academy. As a parting shot before he left, he hacked her medical records and anonymously published the paternity results.

The beginning of his criminal life started with raids on the banking industry. The thin, pale, almost sickly-looking young man with a tuft of bright red hair and blue eyes had amassed a fortune in less than three months. He turned the financial system on its head, and for a brief period of time, there were concerns the commercial markets of Rey-Lin would collapse. Even crime gangs were after him, but they had to take him alive because he had encrypted the accounts so heavily they could not be cracked. He subsequently turned a great deal of his spoils into precious metals and stored them in a secret hideaway he had purchased back on Seltuvay.

Now at the age of twenty-five, he was one of the wealthiest and most wanted men in the solar system. Yukev had tried to visit his family when he received word that his father was dying. Upon returning to their family's farming estate, his mother began screaming at him, and his younger brother—who now towered over him—threatened to kick his ass if he didn't leave. It was a narrow escape as well. His family had contacted the Guard, who seemed to come out of the woodwork shortly after he left. He was able to Quantum Matter Shift off the planet but lost a great deal of wealth when they raided his lair. He ultimately wound up on Ultan deep beneath ground, where he met a woman who told him about a movement trying to overthrow what they believed was a perversely corrupted government. Yukev needed them, and the Libertarium needed him.

Copper ... who the hell uses copper anymore? Yukev muses to himself as he moves quickly to rewire the shuttle. The advent of fiber-optic wiring and quantum processors decades ago makes this ship seem like an old rust bucket to the savvy technician. Tiller had built a working shuttle as a school project when he was only fifteen years old. Unfortunately, he had gotten in trouble for reallocating some sensitive equipment from another lab, and the dean's ground car. But it flew ... well. His schoolmates were amazed he was able to build it so quickly. *Ah the good old days.* The computer wizard longed for a simpler life and swore he would leave this solar system if he survived this ordeal. Suddenly voices shatter his daydream.

"Tiller! *Tiller!* Damn it, snap out of it! How's it coming? We've got to get out of here!"

"This jalopy is old. I'm goin' as fast as I can."

Tosin barks, "Not good enough! Do you want to die?"

"No."

"Then hurry the hell up," the pilot demands before running back down the ramp of the ship.

"Meh-meh-meh, hurry the hell up. Why don't *you* come up here and try wiring this junker from the last century," as he grumbles under his breath. The tech twists the last wire, types in several commands on the keyboard, and suddenly the whir and hum of the power units confirm the vehicle has come to life. Yukev smiles as he slams the wall panel shut and pats the side of the airframe. "Your all mine now, baby."

The slight man hurries down the ramp and shouts to his crewmates, "Okay, we're good to go!"

Zander returns from the other side of the ship and adds, "Got some moh bad news, boss. Looks like grapplin' winch shot. Dat last little numbah done stripped duh return mechanism. We's can grab it. But dats it."

Yukev blurts, "What? Lemme go—"

Tosin breaks in, "No time. They know our last location. We need to get out now. We'll deal with it later. Everyone get in. We're out of here in ten."

Yukev returns to the engine pod and starts to close it up as Zander and Cholash make their way up the ramp. Tosin stops and senses something, then hears explosions in the distance.

He shouts, "Yukev, button it up! They're demoing the caves shut! We've got to go *now*!"

The navigator slams the cover of the engine shut and sprints into the craft. They beeline past the other two convicts in the cargo hold, up the ladder of the flight deck, then hop into their seats. Tosin quickly powers up the engines while Yukev brings the nav system online and displays a map on the windshield in front of them. He informs the pilot, "There's a lava tube right over there that leads out to the other side … unless they blew it up already"

The guardsman lifts the ship up and pushes the yoke forward.

The craft leaps, and he looks over at Yukev. "I thought you said we don't have full power."

Yukev smiles. "We don't. Wait till you see what this baby will do when you get me those parts!"

Tosin shakes his head and grins. The craft screams through the lava tube out into open sky and ascends almost vertically at breakneck speed. Yukev cautions, "Careful 'cause we're gonna guzzle fuel now that I undid the governors."

Tosin acknowledges, "I'll level off and slow down at twenty thousand. Get me some coordinates. Where's that damn ball." The pilot radios, "Zander! Stay frosty! We're probably going to have some company soon."

The gunner acknowledges, "I'm all eyes, boss."

The pilot radios to the large man, "Cholash, grab anything that isn't nailed down. I want to lighten our load."

The large man grabs a rail and heads back to the rear of the cargo ship and begins tearing things out of the wall. Yukev shouts from the flight deck, "Hey! He said only if it's not nailed down. Don't tear the ship apart. I just put it back together!" He turns to the pilot with a concerned look on his face, "Man, that guy's too much!" Tiller adds, "Oh I got a little surprise for you." He pushes several switches, and with a wide, beaming grin, he points at the instrument console, "Ta da!" Boasting, "I turned one of our radars into a scrambler. We can see them … but they can't see us. Instrument flying's gonna be a little limited! Sorry."

The pilot begins to chuckle before saying, "Wow, for a little guy, you're pretty handy … and dangerous!"

Yukev responds, "Okay, looks like number five still has the ball. Heading easterly. So come about two-seventy degrees."

Just then, another set of coordinates comes in.

The navigator corrects, "Nope! Scratch that. New setting is the Lore Jungle. One-zero-niner degrees.

"Copy. One-zero-niner." The pilot makes a hard banking turn.

Cholash now has a pile of junk by the back door and lumbers back up to the cockpit. "Stuff ready. Open door."

Tosin advises, "Oh no. If we have problems, I want you to *throw* it at them."

Cholash looks at Yukev then back at the pilot. He smiles. "Oh! Me starting to like you. Glad no kill."

The crew laughs for a moment. The suns are setting as the number two craft zooms off into the dusky sky.

The warden is now pacing back and forth as he shouts into a device on his wrist, "What do you mean you lost them! How do you lose a prison ship!"

A voice comes through the speaker on the little device. "We're not sure, sir. We suspect they've disabled their tracking device."

The warden seethes under his breath. "Yukev."

The voice queries, "What was that, sir? We couldn't hear you."

Braytire commands, "The coordinates were broadcast for Lore. I want a gauntlet of ships waiting for them. Do you hear me? And if they escape, all of you will wind up as prisoners here in general population. Do you know what will happen then?"

After a brief silence, the voice returns, "Yes, sir. They won't get away this time, sir."

"Frukas out!

The disciplinarian drops back into his chair and wipes his brow. He realizes the population must be going wild with excitement, but he can only think of his family right now. He has to try to do something. He keys some commands into his desk keyboard and overrides the firewalls. "This is Warden Frukas. I need guard command now please."

A voice replies, "Warden, but I—"

"Now!"

"Yes, sir."

After a moment, a second lower voice is heard over the speaker.

"This is command. What can we do for you, Warden? This is highly irregular during the games."

"Yes, yes. I know. I have reason to believe my family may be in danger on Seltuvay. Would you please send a contingent to my estate?"

"Of course, sir. But it will take some time."

"How much time?"

"Could be a half day."

"What! Okay, but please hurry!"

"Copy, sir. Command out."

Faylen Clog is video conferencing with other members of the council as the large vid screen on the wall continues to broadcast the game. A beeping sound starts on his wrist device, and he politely excuses himself and walks briskly out of the main chamber into a side corridor. He looks around to make sure no one is watching before answering the call. "Clog here. What do you want?"

An angry voice blurts out of the small device, and the minister must adjust the volume lower. "I spoke to your warden. He best do his job or his family is dead."

"Why are you calling me? There's nothing I can do."

"This is your fault! Had you not tried to kill me, we wouldn't be having this conversation. And if this goes sideways, mark my words … the galaxy will know what you've done!"

"Dax, we've got it under control. There's no way he'll escape. You're safe … wherever you are, and no one is coming after you. Just sit back and let them do their job. And don't call me anymore. I'm not sure who's monitoring these channels because there's added oversight since the campaign. We need to be careful."

"I don't give a damn who knows. I'm already a criminal—remember? You best beware or I—" Faylen sees someone coming and quickly terminates the call.

"Minister Clog, sorry to disturb you, but you're needed back in the chamber please."

"All right, I will be there shortly. Thank you."

The prime minister composes himself and then proceeds back into the main chamber where a group of citizens are demanding an audience.

After all have left the hallway, a man with a hood covering most of his face steps out from behind a pillar, reaches down, and begins typing onto his wrist com device before turning and quietly stealing away out a side doorway.

Dax is seated behind his large and lavishly carved, dark wooden desk. The newly occupied asteroid has become more a prison than a home as he stares intently at the video screen, awaiting the outcome of the game. New coordinates have been issued, and the remaining ships are proceeding to the Lore Jungle for the next confrontation.

A beeping starts on Dax's wrist device. He answers, "What?"

The voice informs, "Frukas called."

Dax orders, "Take out the father."

"Copy."

A DEADLY JUNGLE

The number five ship streams along with the Drothamae nestled snugly underneath the outside of the ship. The display now shows only sixteen hours left. The number one, four, eight, and ten crafts are following in pursuit, and the lead ship is evading sporadic laser fire coming from the followers as they all enter the thick canopy of the jungle in the dead of night. The pilot of the number five ship has extended his lead, and extinguishes its lights before hiding in a cave behind a waterfall while the other ships go racing by. While all the ships have radar, it is limited and with the stealth capabilities of the shuttles, it adds to the excitement by including a deadly form of hide-and-seek.

Tosin and company enter the jungle a short while later. But unlike the other ships, Yukev's modifications on their instruments clearly show the craft hidden behind the waterfall, even in the blackness of the dense forest. He slows the ship in front of the cascade and turns it around so that its rear is facing the water. As the other ship doesn't realize they have been spotted, they lie in wait and power up their weapons. Tosin opens the ramp of their ship while Cholash holds onto a handrail with one hand and a large piece of metal in the other. The pilot begins to reverse toward the other ship and shouts, "Now!"

Cholash heaves the large metal rod like a spear, which slams squarely into the front windshield of the ship. He closes the door quickly. The pilot of the number five craft attempts to evade them, but Zander trains a flurry of laser fire on the starboard engine, and the ship lurches and begins to fall. The Drothamae is jarred loose and falls into the water below. Tosin quickly maneuvers their ship away from the waterfall, and with the other ship crippled, Tosin commands Zander again over their com, "Okay, let 'em have it. Both barrels!" Zander's eyes are wide and maniacal as he unloads salvo after salvo on the ship until it finally falls onto the jungle floor, and bursts into a grand explosion. The ball sits at the bottom of the waterfall with its large timer still counting down. Tosin now slowly brings the ship into the same location behind the waterfall and lies in wait.

Yukev asks curiously, "Aren't you gonna get the ball?"

Tosin shakes his head and says, Quiet. It's bait. Let them all fight over it. No chatter."

The number one and eight ships return and begin a pitched battle to retrieve the ball. Hovering around each other in a deadly dance, they unleash a flurry of laser and pulse cannon bursts at each other. The number one ship sustains damage and retreats deep into the jungle. Tosin recedes even further into the cave behind the waterfall careful to keep their ship hidden from the vehicles outside. Small drones that follow around the Drothamae are broadcasting the game. So far, Tosin has been able to remain undetected by the cameras. The number eight ship surveys the wreckage of the other at the bottom of the waterfall before launching its grappling claw. It clamps onto the top of the Drothamae and the heavy metal cable retracts it up into the indentation underneath the craft. The number ten shuttle dives in and begins shooting at the number eight vessel, which now has the ball firmly in place. The new defender dodges the incoming fire and peels off in the opposite direction. It heads for the coordinates in the center of the jungle with the number ten ship following in pursuit.

Braytire is lurched forward, staring at the screen and wondering what just happened. He thought he saw the number two ship momentarily, but in the midst of all the havoc, he cannot tell if it was a glitch or they were destroyed. He contacts the field major. "Did you see them?"

The voice answers, "It all happened before we could get there. We think we saw them on the screen, but—"

The warden interrupts, "Survey the wreckage. I need an answer now!"

"Yes, Warden. Back in ten."

The chief jailer leans back in his chair, now worried about his family.

Seltuvay, a sister planet of Sulimay, still retains the lush beauty that Kree, its small moon, lost. Grand castles lie atop purple mountains. Plains and grasslands are populated by large farms responsible for feeding the population of Rey-Lin. Braytire Frukas owns a large estate on the coast by one of the planet's oceans, and although he is away a great deal of the time, his relatives live there. He has no wife or child due to his work as a warden, but with two other brothers and a sister, there are plenty of children happily running around. His mother and father live there as well. The mansion is sprawling, with twelve bedrooms, fifteen baths, courts for sports, and a large swimming pool. None are cramped. The large family enjoys getting together and going out on long hikes to stay healthy as well as picnics on the beach below.

After landing their ship a short distance away, a contingent of guards marches swiftly in formation toward the main gate. The officer in charge knocks on the large metal door, sending an echo throughout the structure. After a moment, a man who looks strikingly like an older version of the warden but with longer and darker ash-blonde hair answers, "Yes? Can I help you, sir?"

The guard responds, "Sorry for the intrusion, sir, but Warden Frukas insisted we send some men here for your safety. It seems there's been a threat to your family."

Lentor Frukas, father of the warden, moves his son aside and scoffs, "Nonsense! What fool would have the audacity to attempt anything on this family?"

A mercenary now perched over two kilometers to the north on top of one of the many cliffs that line the shoreline has a clear shot and takes it from a highly modified sniper rifle. The bullet possesses a guidance system, and once the target has been acquired, it is almost impossible to evade it. The guard captain who is talking to him happens to move in front of the man as the explosive projectile comes whistling in. The round blows his head clean off then continues on to blast a hole through the Lentor's skull. The son is spattered in blood and recoils in horror at the sight of the headless soldier and the gaping chasm in his father's head as the lifeless bodies drop to the ground with collective thuds. He crumples to the floor while the guards surround the door in a semicircle and assume a defensive posture. The second in command barks orders to other men, "Get them inside and secure!" then hails the pilot and navigator still left in their ship, "Transport liftoff and do a sweep of the cliffs north of our position!"

The pilot responds, "Copy."

Before the ship can get ten meters in the air, a rocket-propelled grenade screams in from another section of the cliff, and the transport explodes in a ball of fire.

The second in command sees the fireball and immediately radios for help, "Orbital, orbital. We are under attack! Say again we are under attack! Two down. Transport destroyed. Suspect rock face north of our location. Need immediate suppression and evac."

A voice comes through on his headset. "Copy—suppress and evac. Remain under cover. Secondary transport in ten."

Within a short period of time, powerful pulse cannons from the orbiting ship decimate the rock face, and reduce a section of the cliff into a large pile of rubble that tumbles into the sea below in a matter of seconds. There is now a crater etched out of the serene rock face from where the mercenaries attacked, and Dax probably knew it would be a suicide mission for them.

Inside, the family gathers in an interior safe room, and all are weeping at the loss of their patriarch. The son who witnessed the attack is in shock as the new lead officer tries to console him, "Mr.

Frukas, I am so sorry for your loss. But you need to concentrate. We have to get you all out of here. It's not safe. Is there a back door or escape route out of here?"

He is shivering and cannot speak as the other brother comes over and demands, "Who the hell would've done this? What did Braytire do?"

The head guard repeats himself, "Sir, we need to leave. Is there another way out?"

The second brother confirms, "Yes, there is a trap door in the study that leads to steps going down under ground and coming out by the beach."

The guard responds, "Thank you. Okay, please collect up your family and let's get moving. I'm not sure if there will be another attempt."

The guards assist the rest of the family, a great deal of them still crying, and all shuffle quickly into the study. Once there, the brothers both remove a table and throw rug in the center of the room to reveal a large door cut into the wooden floor. It takes two of the men to pull the heavy steel covering up. It creaks and whines as it opens, and a dark staircase is revealed below. One of the brothers walks several steps down, flicks some switches at a panel on the side of the stairway, and lights illuminate the void below. All start to descend the steep stairs, and the lead guard makes a final call to his comrades in space, "Stairwell in center of compound. Egress to beach. Will blow smoke for LZ when there."

A voice acknowledges, "Copy beach egress. We are sending armed escort as well. Be careful."

"Thanks. Ground team out."

Braytire Frukas sits in his chair weeping. He has just received the news of the attack at his estate on Seltuvay and his father's death. He swears under his breath, "Maytor Dax will pay for this," but he can't do anything yet, so as not to risk being discovered. He steadies himself and summons an aide.

A slender man dressed in black with a cap and boots enters the room and stands at attention in front of the warden. He inquires, "Yes, sir, what can I do for you?"

The warden seems exhausted and in a somber tone inquires, "What is the current status?"

The aide snaps, "As you can see on the screen, based on the information from the drones, the number eight shuttle now possesses the Drothamae after destroying the number five ship. The number one, four and ten shuttles are in pursuit, and they all just passed the checkpoint in the Lore Jungle. The new coordinates have been issued, and all are heading toward the Treydan Polar Cap.

"What about the number two ship?" the warden inquires.

"The survey teams are still assessing the damage. It was pretty bad. There is a pile of steel burnt beyond recognition on the jungle floor. Completely destroyed. We think there was a battle before the drones arrived, and the number two ship was destroyed as well. They are doing dental scans now on the skeletons to see who was lost."

"Send some additional troops to shadow the remaining ships."

"Sir?"

"Just … do it … *please!*"

"Yes, sir. Right away, sir."

The aide spins on his heels and exits the room quickly while initiating a call on his wrist device.

The warden whispers under his breath while staring at the screen, "Damn it, Luval. Where the hell are you?"

The crew of the number two ship has been silent for a while. They set the craft down shortly after the survey ships arrived and now lie in wait for them to leave. Yukev whispers to Tosin, "We can't stay here forever. We're gonna have to get out eventually."

The pilot snaps under his breath, "Quiet! Keep your mouth shut. Looks like they're almost done."

A guardsman down below finishes scanning the wreckage and reports back in, "This is survey one. We've confirmed the number five crew. There's no sign of the number two ship. Awaiting further instructions."

"A voice returns, "Stand by for orders survey one."

After a moment, the voice adds, "Okay return to base. But bring the bodies … or what's left of them with you."

The guard complains, "But they're in pieces!"

"Warden wants them brought back."

The guard shakes his head and responds, "Copy base."

As the other men begin to collect the remains, there is a rustling in the bush, followed by a gurgling sound. A large beast with huge fangs and leathery scales leaps out of the trees and stands nearly three meters tall. It lets out a blood-curdling scream and devours the two men whole before they can open fire. The other three guardsmen try to run back to the ship, but the beast swats all of them against a tree and then rips them apart with the huge talons sticking out of its hands. After it's savage feast, the monster washes it down with a long drink out of the pool underneath the waterfall. It stops and looks up toward the cascading water.

Tosin and the rest of them hold their breath, suspecting that it can sense them. Yukev nudges the pilot and whispers, "I think it's time to go." The large animal sits back on its haunches and is ready to leap. The pilot has already powered up the engines and blasts through the waterfall and barely escapes the leaping beast.

Cholash comments, "Kragor. Used to have one as pet. Got too big and had to kill. Me sad. Loved it much."

Zander questions, "A pet? You had one of them for a pet?"

"Mmmm. Rescued as baby. Loved it. But got too big."

Yukev turns to Tosin. "Okay new destination is Treydan."

Tosin inquires, "The Polar Cap?"

Yukev nods. "Yup."

"How's our fuel?"

The navigator informs, "Not good. Only ten thousand left."

Tosin banks the ship back around toward the pool.

Yukev complains, "What are you doing now?"

"Getting some gas."

"But—"

"We'll do a survey. If it's gone, we do a quick salvage and dust off. We *need* the fuel and we might as well salvage some other supplies. If we do it right, we can be out of there in ten. Get ready to hook up the fueling hose. Zander, Cholash? Get as many of the laser and cannon packs as you can carry. I'll put the ship into hover mode and man the guns from here in case that ... thing comes back."

The rest of the crew looks at each other, shrug, and answer in unison, "Okay."

The ship descends and banks hard in the direction of the large pile. There are blood and body parts everywhere, revealing the grotesqueness of the preceding massacre. The other shuttle, now a heap of metal, is still smoldering as the guard ship sits quiet and undisturbed save for some gashes in the side from the beast as it left. Tosin cautions, "Okay, let's do this fast."

The others leap out of the open cargo ramp in the rear of the ship. Cholash and Zander try their best not to step on what's left of the bodies and enter the guard ship through the rear ramp. Yukev spies the fueling hose of the red ship and tugs on it quickly. The slender and somewhat pasty-skinned man attaches it to a port on the stubby wing of their shuttle. He comes around to the front and signals up to Tosin with a thumbs-up gesture to begin fueling. Tosin flips a switch and hears the pumps begin to whine. Yukev speaks into a wrist device, which he has now connected to the main communications of their ship, and adds, "I'm going into the guard ship."

Tosin complains, "We don't have time!"

Yukev offers, "I want to check something."

Tosin demands, "Be careful."

He runs past Zander and Cholash, who have their arms full of supplies and are returning to their ship. As they reach the bottom, Yukev comes around in front of them, holds up his hands and shouts, "Stop!"

Cholash belts, "We must go! No time."

Yukev contacts Tosin on his com unit. "Tosin! Stop the pumps!"

The pilot screams, "We have to get out of here!"

Yukev replies, "Yeah but on *that* ship," pointing to the referee shuttle.

The pilot is quiet for a second, then responds, "What's the condition?"

"It's great! Full armaments. The beast didn't do that much damage, *and* we have orbital capability. We can get off this rock now!"

"I'm reversing the pumps and then coming over to you."

Yukev runs down the ramp, looks at Zander and Cholash, and excitedly commands, "Put it back, boys. We got a new ride."

Zander looks at the large man, back to Yukev, then rolls his eyes before complaining, "Why y'all say nothin' foh dis? Imma stahtin' get tired uh dis mess."

Cholash adds, "Me hungry."

Yukev comforts, "There's tons of rations in there, big guy. Put the stuff back and go chow down. And it's the good stuff too, not that crap they give us!"

Cholash remarks, "Oh?" before turning and lumbering back up the ramp.

Tosin sprints up the ramp and looks at Yukev. "Can you hack it?"

"Already did."

"Okay let's get out of here."

"We gotta disconnect the fuel hose."

Cholash volunteers, "I do it. But want food when done."

Tosin looks at him. "Deal. Zander, can you grab a couple of those bodies and throw them on our ship?"

"What! Oh man, deys in pieces!"

"Just grab up whatever you can and throw it in the cargo hold. Hurry up!"

"I didn't sign up foh dis. Dat's jus down right nasty."

Tosin reminds him, "Do you want get off this rock … or not?"

Zander shrugs, "Yeah okay … but dang … dat jus wrong."

The large man runs down the ramp and over to the fuel hose while Tosin and Yukev prep the ship for takeoff. Yukev types furiously on the keyboard, then looks at the pilot. "Okay, we're in. Number two ship is now under remote control."

Zander throws multiple pieces of human bodies into their old ship, punches the knob to close the ramp, then scuffles back onto the red guard ship. Cholash is undoing the fuel hose when the Kragor jumps out from the trees and swipes at the man. He turns and stares straight at the beast. It stands on its hind legs, and is about to pounce on Cholash, who grabs a large metal pipe and wedges it into the ground. The monster comes down, and is impaled by the spire while the big convict moves out of the way. It lets out a huge howl as Cholash runs to the back of the ship. The monster pulls the pipe out of its chest and begins to follow. Zander trains a pulse cannon on the beast and blows its head off with one shot. He comments, "Hey, boss, I tink deese got moh pep dan ours do."

Cholash is almost to the ramp when another slightly smaller Kragor leaps out from the bush and grabs the large man. He tries to break free, but the monster tears his head off like a small treat.

Tiller screams to the pilot, "There's a second one. Get outta here now!"

The red craft leaps off the jungle floor, comes around, and launches two missiles. A large explosion consumes the beast, their old ship and the existing wreckage. Tosin points the craft north toward the ice sheets and punches the throttle.

Yukev hops into the seat, and Zander comes up the ladder in between them, out of breath, and complains, "Cholash didn't deserve goin' out dat way. We shoulda done sumfin'."

Yukev turns back to him and challenges, "Like what? That thing took his head off before I could even get a gun on him. It's over, okay? At least he died quickly. Now let's get outta here." He turns to face the pilot and in a mildly concerned voice informs, "Uh, Tosin, space is *that* way," as he points up at the sky.

The pilot replies curtly, "Not yet."

The navigator sits back in his seat and muses, "Why did I know you were gonna say that. Okay, now what?"

The System Guard has storage depots all over this rock. Right?"

Yukev pecks at the keyboard and a red circle appears on the holographic map between them. He confirms, "The closest one is near the south pole by the Seydan Ice Sheet."

"Ok bundle up. We're taking a detour. It's going to get chilly."

The pilot banks hard and pushes the throttle forward causing the engines to roar. The ship streaks toward the South Pole in the dead of night.

Faylen Clog leans forward in his chair, and views the image of Warden Frukas on a screen in front of him on his large wooden desk.

There is a pause before Frukas complains, "That bastard Dax murdered my father!"

Faylen tries to console him, "Braytire, I am deeply sorry for your lose. I—"

"Things have gotten out of control prime minister," cautions the jailer.

"Why can't you just blow them up?" queries Clog.

The warden replies in an exasperated tone, "Their ship *is* blown up, but we haven't located the bodies yet. I assure you, sir, if they are still alive, they will be dealt with. Even if they are, they can't have gone too far in that jungle in the dead of night. Hopefully they'll get mauled or eaten by a Kragor. I have a hundred men out there looking for them. But we still have the game to deal with."

Faylen Clog responds, "Call me immediately if there are any updates."

The warden vows, "Faylen ... when this is over, Dax is done ... either by you ... or *me!*

The prime minister finishes, "Agreed. Clog out," before hitting a button on the console on his desk and terminating the call.

The twin suns of Rey and Lin are beginning to rise as Tosin pushes the referee ship to its limit to reach the depot on the southern pole of Drotham by the edge of a large glacier known as the Seydan Ice Sheet. Yukev Tiller complains, "Hey we're gorging fuel."

"I don't care. We only need to make it to the depot. Do we have enough to get there?"

"Yeah, but at this speed, just barely. We didn't have time to top-off before."

"I want to stock up on ammo and we can refuel while we're there as well. Shouldn't take that long." Tosin takes the ship into a steep dive and circles down to a metal building with a corrugated roof that is almost completely hidden under a snowdrift. The ship creates a large puff of snow as it lands gently in front of the structure.

Tiller stares out at the half covered storehouse and cautions, "These depots have major security and will blow if we trip the alarm".

"Does everything on this planet blow up?"

The tech responds dryly, "Yeah ... pretty much."

The three fugitives creep slowly up to a side door, and Yukev disengages the security lock then delicately coaxes it open. The convicts enter cautiously and Tiller warns, "Don't touch anything until I give the all-clear. Okay?" The other two nod in compliance. As they walk down a line of shelves stocked with various boxes, a hail of pulse rounds greets them, and they dive behind some crates.

A female voice emanates from behind a large wall of metal containers and demands, "Who are you and what do you want!"

Tosin instantly recognizes the voice. A mercenary from Ultan that he had put away a year ago, she had been difficult to track and even harder to catch. Jenidayah Horn was a skilled warrior who left the guard suddenly after years of service and turned to freelance work. The High Council had labeled her a traitor, and her records were sealed. She had claimed innocence, and even though the evidence of her crime was marginal at best, no one would listen. Jenidayah was convicted of murder and sent to the women's prison on Drotham. Tosin now wonders if maybe he was wrong about her and she *was* telling the truth.

The pilot replies, "Jenidayah Horn, does Warden Martanique know you're out taking a stroll in the snow?"

"That voice, I *know* that voice. Tosin Luval, the disgraced war hero. Well … ha ha … *now* do you believe the High Council is dirty?"

Luval attempts to reason with her, "Jen, let's talk. I'm throwing out my weapon. We don't have much time, and we have a plan. I can get you off this rock!"

Another flurry of laser fire pins Tosin down as he hides deeper behind the crates, now smoldering from her deadly barrage. "Oh no you don't. Sweet-talking me just like you did last t—"

Tosin cuts her off. "Have you seen any of the broadcast? We're being *hunted*! I'm not here for you."

Yukev points at his com unit and whispers loudly, "We don't have time for this."

Tosin puts up his hand and acknowledges before speaking again. "Look, they have my wife and kid holed up on some asteroid. The Libert—"

Jen interrupts, "The *Libertarium*? They haven't done *squat* for me. I did two jobs for them, and they left me for dead. Screw them!"

Tosin continues to plead with the woman, "Jen, please stop! We are on the same side. We can help you."

Another barrage erupts from her weapon as she blankets Tosin's location with a flurry of particle energy that is reducing everything around him into small bits of metal.

"I've heard all your crap before, Luval!" she screams, "This could just as easily be a trap you concocted with the High Council!"

Yukev radios into his com bracelet, "I'm going to flank her, but she's not going to give up easily. Please be ready. I don't want this bitch taking me out before we've finished this mess. Okay?"

"Copy," acknowledges the pilot in a whisper.

Tosin dives behind another container as she unleashes another round of mayhem from her gun. Tiller eases up behind her and touches the barrel to forehead. She quickly turns to strike him, but he fires a weapon in his other hand at her torso, and she drops with a grunt. She tries to stand, and the nerd unloads two more rounds that lay her down flat onto her stomach and unconscious. Yukev kicks her weapon away and quickly zip-ties her arms and legs while Tosin runs over and kneels in front of her.

"Did you kill her?" Tosin protests.

"No, but I had to hit her three times on stun. She's a beast!"

"Okay, let's get her in the ship and get out of here."

"What?" scream both Zander and Yukev in unison. "Are you crazy?"

The pilot responds, "She can help if I can reason with her."

"And if not?" questions Tiller.

"Then I'll end her myself."

Yukev and Zander begin grabbing packages and stuffing them into bags. After Luval applies programmable restraints to her, he flips her wiry but toned frame over his shoulder and carries her out of the depot and up into the ship. Once secured to the bulkhead, he sits and watches her as she regains consciousness. She meets his eyes with a cold stare and opines, "They're never gonna let you go."

He hurries back down the ramp, attaches a hose to the side of the shuttle, and begins pumping fuel.

Tiller runs out to find Tosin staring into the gray sky and

excitedly holds up a container with a large grin on his pale, waifish face. "Nano-wrap!"

The pilot tilts his head with a confused look. "What?"

"Nano-wrap. Programmable paint. This place has a vat of it!"

"I'm still not following you." Tosin struggles to understand.

Yukev is slightly agitated that he has to explain but continues, "We can paint the ship, and then we can be whatever we want. A shuttle … a referee ship … a guard cruiser … with a keystroke!"

The pilot realizes the deception and immediately smiles at his partner. They both return inside to wheel the machinery outside. Tosin adds, "I think there's a storm coming."

Yukev advises, "This stuff dries on contact, so we should be okay if I get it on quickly."

The tech punches in some keystrokes on a panel on the side of the large tank, and the nozzle begins applying the compound to the hull of the shuttle.

Luval complains, "It's white!"

"That's because it's dormant while it's being applied. When it's done, it'll be whatever color you want. It even has some shape-shifting qualities. We can't really *change* the shape of the ship, but it does some freaky things with reflections. Makes it look like a different craft. Pretty amazing actually," Yukev adds admiringly.

"They're probably going to broadcast new coordinates pretty soon, so I'm heading up onto the flight deck." Tosin turns and heads back up the ramp of the ship.

It takes Yukev a half hour to finish spraying the entire craft. He walks back over to a tablet lying on an oil drum, keys in a couple of commands, and the vehicle turns bright pink. Zander is walking out with a last cache of supplies and sees the color.

He complains, "Oh hell no!"

Tiller has a smirk on his face, and after keying a few more taps on the device, the ship returns to the red referee color.

The black man's eyes are wide open as he stares in amazement. "Really? Y'all can do dat?"

Yukev beams a smile and pats the man on the shoulder. "All that and a cup of coffee, my brother. Get on board. I gotta contact some people on Kree."

The ship rises and seems to float on a white cloud of snow before disappearing into the cloudy morning sky.

THE LIBERTARIUM

Kree was once a beautiful moon, full of lush foliage and deep blue oceans. But industry decimated the little celestial body. Between illegal mining and the pollution it's generated, the small world has become a brown, dead rock. There are many gambling establishments and brothels for sex. The main spaceport is decrepit, and most of the ships are in disrepair. There is, however, another private facility exclusively for use by large companies and illegal cartels, where vessels of all shapes and sizes are cared for by top-notch crews who keep them clean and in perfect condition. The rest of the small rock is filled with prostitutes, addicts, and visitors wanting to partake in the sordid activities offered on the planet. Many of the beings on Kree are trapped—victims of the vices that brought them here. Others are indentured servants of the cartels, either captured slaves or souls too poor to make it on their own. Regardless, the general population is as destitute as the world is dead.

But there is also a hidden faction here. A group not aligned with the government, hiding deep in obscurity—with people on the other planets as well, waging a relentless war on the cartels surreptitiously.

No one knows their true identity or where they come from except for their name, the *Libertarium*. It is thought that the secret and skilled spies that lurk in the shadows were members of the guard at one time or another. Dax's men have never been able to find them, and the thugs that have fallen, died a slow and painful death by methods said to be even more barbaric than those of the cartels. Many of Dax's minions complain that they are genuinely more fearful of this murky force than the System Guard itself, which at this point has become half-corrupt. But their mission, while vigilante in nature, is said to be sincere: to wage war on the corruption now crippling the Rey-Lin system.

The room is dark, and the air dank. The walls are adorned with pictures of past celebrity patrons, but they are all faded and barely visible. A bartender is wiping down the bar of the mostly empty establishment on Kree. A man and woman are seated at one of the few tables in the tavern. The room is not very big and a video screen on the wall displays the ongoing game of Drothamae, with numbers and odds on the side of the screen. Betting on the game is a very popular pastime, and many have made, or lost, a great deal of money on the outcome. The door opens to reveal a hooded man who enters and walks toward them. He sits and pulls back his hood to reveal a long mane of fire-red hair above a heavily tattooed and pierced face. The woman queries, "Well?"

"It's just as we thought. Clog is in bed with Dax. The whole thing was set up. Luval was framed."

The woman leans forward, and the dim light above reveals long white dreadlocks over a weathered but still attractive face. Her blue-gray eyes train on the redhead. She is silent for a long moment before responding, "That's it then. Justice must be administered. Advise our friends on Seltuvay we may need an extraction force for the major but he will need to hold out until we can get to him. What about the council?"

"Reital is suspicious but has no proof yet. Tumarian is a pawn, so he is useless. The rest of them are unaware of the situation, and we believe they are innocent."

"Then Clog will need to be dealt with off-world away from the guard. And Frukas?"

"Not sure. He could be swayed. We have intel that Dax had his father murdered. He's still taking orders from Clog right now, but that could change. And the game is turning into a mess. One thing's for sure. If Luval wins, there are going to be a couple of really rich people out of this one. Have you seen the odds?"

"Irrelevant. Braytire will need to go as well."

"Contact Tiller on Drotham and update him on the plan. We don't have much time. Dax?"

"Holed up somewhere in the Gureeg Asteroid Belt. We can't get an exact location because the cartel has set up a wide-area interference field. The whole cluster is scrambled."

The woman looks down pensively for a moment before suggesting, "Then we will need a recon mission. Take a ship and see if you can pinpoint his location. There will be several escorts guarding the main base, but he probably has a few placed as decoys to throw people off as well. And be careful; if we're caught, it will jeopardize the entire operation."

"What about Luval's family?"

"Most likely Dax has them. Once you have his location, we'll send a team. They're already waiting to go."

The redheaded man puts his hood back on, rises from the table, then heads back out of the tavern quickly. The woman turns toward the bar and puts up her arm. The bartender spies the gesture and motions toward a computer on the side, and begins to type on the keyboard. The barman then brings over a large stein of frothy dark brown liquid and places it down on the table, nodding ever so slightly to confirm that the woman's earlier request has been sent. Her bodyguard, who has been quiet up until now, grabs the large glass and draws a long swallow before putting it back down on the worn table. The woman turns to him and directs, "I need you to go back to Ultan. I will return shortly but I have an errand first."

The man protests, "M'lady Na'edra! I swore an oath to give my life to protect you. I—"

The woman cuts him off. "My devoted Uleen, I have spent many years in combat and in the shadows. I will be fine. I need you to get a message back to our headquarters, and I don't want to do it electronically." She scribbles a cryptic sentence on a napkin. "Take this and go … now."

The man with a dark complexion and curly black hair finishes his drink and wipes some foam from his thick beard and moustache before standing to reveal his towering two-and-a-half-meter height. He bows before speaking in a deep tone. "I will do as you ask but will not feel at ease until you are safely home."

She looks up at him with a sympathetic gaze that seems maternal in nature and smiles. She holds, and then pats his large hand in reassurance. After the bodyguard leaves, she bows her head and thinks to herself, *The Libertarium must succeed!*

WARRIOR PRINCESS

s Jenidayah tries to undo the restraints, the femme fatale thinks about her past. The exterior of her home world, Ultan, is quite warm. As the closest planet to the binary stars of Rey and Lin, the surface temperature of five hundred degrees scorches everything. It is a barren rock void of anything but volcanoes belching lava. Vast cities, however, have been hollowed out of the interior, hundreds of meters below the scalding surface. The abundance of geothermal energy and aquifers of liquid water deep in the crust sustain a large population. Precious minerals are mined and exported throughout the rest of the solar system. Oddly, this heap of slightly molten rock is the richest in the system. The wealthier areas of this subterranean settlement are outfitted with large projection arrays that bathe the high ceilings with vistas of blue sky and distant mountains. Certain public areas are designed to look like sunbathed ocean shores or lush jungles. Vast hydroponic farms are used to grow food for the entire population. The fiery planet belies the underground oasis that was created on such a hellish world.

Jenidayah lived a sheltered princess's life. Her father was a senior administrator of the mining conglomerate, and her mother sat on the board of regents—the planetary council governing Ultan. The little girl had only been off world a handful of times before the accident that tore her from her home world and turned her life upside down forever. It was an earthquake. A big one. While they were a normal part of life on a cosmic body with active tectonic plates, this temblor had been one for the ages. Jenidayah had been away at camp on Flon D'Mar, the antithesis of Ultan. The distant world is covered by water on seventy percent of the planet. The sun is weaker that far out, and it is colder—except at the equator, where she attended a summer camp. Jenidayah's parents wanted her to experience naturally fresh air and the freedom of being on the surface as opposed to underground.

Ultan has advanced warning sensors and a very comprehensive safety protocol, but no one had expected the catastrophe that occurred that day. A recent eruption from one of the largest volcanoes started a cascading effect on the fault lines that shook the entire planet. After the final tally was done, eleven million souls had been lost in a span of five hours as the shaking collapsed three of the five major underground cities. Jenidayah's family and home were entombed for eternity. She never got over the loss. She was passed from communal homes to foster care, and by sixteen years of age, her anger had consumed her.

It was a meeting with a grief counselor that pointed her to the System Guard. Jenidayah had been a brilliant student academically, but rage burned in her like the surface of Ultan. She soon rose through the ranks of the Guard to lieutenant. However, her penchant for getting in trouble or not following orders soon became her undoing. She grew to be a stunning woman with a long, brown mane of curly hair that bordered her well-featured face. High cheekbones underneath deep brown piercing eyes and a pug nose atop the full lips of her wide mouth complemented her well-built body and light brown skin. Jenidayah left the military and became a mercenary for hire to the highest bidder. She had grown cold and calculated; shutting the memories off was the only way she could stomach the terrible things she had done. Many of her jobs had been to dispatch criminals by rival criminals. She had never hurt or killed an innocent. That had been one of her cardinal rules. But Dax tried to deceive her with a contract for her last assassination.

The warrior woman had always been suspicious of the crime boss, and after some research, realized the mark was an innocent man, but the thug wanted his land. He had refused to sell, so Dax wanted him killed. She declined the job, but several days later the man and his family were murdered. Maytor then framed her by planting evidence at the crime scene pointing to her involvement, and a warrant was issued for her arrest. Tosin had discovered her hiding at a resort on Sulimay. After an intense chase, the two fought a pitched battle on a sun-soaked beach that had left them both bloodied. The girl, skilled in both hand to hand and weapons training, slashed at Tosin with her curved sword but the major was able to outwit her with a wrestling move that wrapped her up and rendered her defenseless—capturing and arresting her while tourists looked on in fear. Jenidayah pleaded innocent but had an inexperienced lawyer. Once the discovery of her mercenary endeavors had come to light, she was convicted and sent to Drotham for life. She could never bring that family back, but swore she would find a way to get even with Dax … and Luval.

Tosin looks over at Yukev and says, "Hey, I need to talk to Jenidayah. I'm putting the ship on autopilot, but can you just stay up here and watch out for any unwanted guests please?"

"Yeah sure," replies Tiller. "But you better watch out for her. I just got everything stabilized with the ship."

"She's a damn good gunner. We could use her, and I think she's innocent. Just let me try."

Tiller reminds him, "Remember what you said."

The pilot gets up from the chair and straps on one of the side arms they stole from the dead guardsmen in the Lore Jungle. He then hits a button on the side of the weapon, and a bleep confirms the safety is off while continuing to stare at his copilot.

He climbs down the ladder and walks through the cargo hold toward Jenidayah, who is still restrained but talking to Zander.

"Hey, Zander, can you give me a moment with her?"

Zander responds, "Yeah, boss, I told her a li'l story. Say you framed. We friends now."

Tosin smiles. "Thanks Zander. Give me a minute, okay?"

Zander gets up moves back up toward the flight deck.

Jenidayah stares up at the pilot and states, "So you sweet-talked them too, huh?"

"Jen, c'mon. What do I have to do to prove it to you?"

"Oh, I dunno, take these restraints off so I can choke you to death. Why didn't you just leave me at the depot?"

"Because I think you were framed by the same people that got me. And I believe it goes all the way up to top. Someone on the council is in bed with Dax. My mission was level five, top secret, and he still found out."

The woman retorts, "Doesn't matter because we're screwed. It's only a matter of time before they find out about your little charade, and then … *boom.* We all go up. Thanks for including me in your death sentence."

Tiller hops down from the flight deck, runs up to them, and interrupts, "Hey, I got in touch with them."

Tosin inquires, "Them?"

"Yeah, the Libertarium."

Jenidayah complains, "Oh great, just what we need. They're half the reason I'm here. You think I'm gonna trust them?"

Yukev insists, "They hacked the files. They've got Clog talking to Dax!"

Luval scratches his head. "So what … you're a triple agent?"

"Well … I did a couple of jobs for them but didn't really get too involved until I was here. Look, it's good news. We can beat this."

The guardsman stands and raises his voice. "Dax has my family! They can't broadcast anything yet, or my wife and child are dead!"

Tiller tries to reassure him, "They've got a team on the way. They know where your family is. I wanted to cut and run, but they instructed me to tell you to continue playing the game. We need to stall them for time."

Jenidayah massages her hands, having gotten free while they were talking, and Tosin draws his weapon and points it at her head. She quickly puts her hands up and shouts, "Whoa there, cowboy! I didn't realize the *kidnapped wife and child* story was true. I'm still pissed you caught me, but I'll help," as she puts out her hand to him.

Zander, who has moved back over to them, comments, "Shake da girl's hand now. G'on! I'm tired a listenin' all dis crap, man!"

Tosin holsters the sidearm and shakes Jenidayah's hand.

"So now what?" she inquires.

Tosin answers, "Now we win and get off this rock. Both of you get on guns. Jen, when it's time, I'd like you to man the grappler. Okay, let's get to work."

The pilot and navigator return to the cockpit while Zander and Jenidayah stow the material from the guard depot they just pillaged.

Jenidayah comments, "Damn, you guys just about cleaned that place out!"

"Mmm … better us dan dem," responds Zander.

Zander adds, "Ya know, comes to think of it, all dis fightin' got me hungry. How 'bout you, li'l lady? You hungry? Maybe I whip us up some fixin's." He pulls some packets out of one of the storage cabinets in the wall.

Jenidayah complains, "Ugh, I'm sick of those MREs."

He brags with a big grin and eyes wide, "Ah but wait 'til you tastes what I does wit 'em … ha ha."

Zander sets up a small cooking unit on the cargo bay floor and begins mixing some of the packets together. Within several minutes, he has made a stew with an aroma that floats through the entire ship. Yukev stops what he is doing in the cockpit and casts a curious look over at Tosin. "Do you smell that?"

The pilot replies, "Yeah."

Yukev is about to unharness himself when Jenidayah climbs up the ladder into the cockpit with two steaming bowls.

"Zander thought you might be hungry. I'm not sure how he turned rations into this stew, but it's pretty tasty."

Tiller quickly spins and grabs one of the bowls. He takes a slurp and looks at Tosin with a surprised grin. Luval turns and stares at Jenidayah. He reaches for the bowl, and she pulls it away. "I should let you starve. I'm still pissed at you for turning me in."

She pushes the bowl towards him, and the steaming liquid nearly spills out before turning quickly and descending back down the ladder.

"Boy you're really at the top of her list, huh?" opines the navigator.

Tosin nods as he switches the controls to autopilot and begins to eat. Yukev, almost choking, pauses for a moment from gobbling his food and types in a request on his keyboard. A holographic map is displayed in front of them, with a blinking red dot showing the present location of the ball.

"We're gonna need to make up some time."

Tosin concurs and leans forward and hits a button on his console, and the ship lurches forward. He answers dryly, "Super cruise engaged."

Yukev types another command, and the nose of the ship out the windshield seems to disappear as he adds, "Now we're hot and dark."

A WATERY GRAVE

As the prisoners scream north to narrow the distance between them and the other shuttles, new coordinates splatter across the cockpit windshield. Yukev feels his heart jump as he stares at the numbers blinking in red. He turns to his pilot and starts shaking his head.

Tosin asks, "What's wrong?"

Yukev complains, "The Dreader Trench. It's the deepest damn place on Drotham!"

"So?"

Yukev quickly types in some commands on the keypad, and a holographic map reappears between them. He points at their present location and informs, "The good news is we can turnaround. Bad news is,"—he motions to a position on the map in the southwestern ocean. "This is the trench. *Underwater!* The pressure down there is ridiculous! I'm not sure we can handle it."

"What about the paint?"

"It's not the paint I'm worried about. We'll keep a tight seal, but this ship still took a hit from that Kragor. If the bulkheads warp, we'll be crushed like a can. It's too risky."

"Okay, then we shadow them at a hundred meters."

Tiller agrees and adds, "We're configured for radar evasion, but if you can find some fish, try and stay inside the school or pod or whatever it is they call them."

Tosin nods and then banks the ship hard right and takes them out over the ocean. He suggests, "You may want to go back and prepare everyone. Make sure they have their environmental suits on in case it starts to get damp."

The copilot jumps out of his chair, hurries down the ladder off the flight deck, and heads down the narrow hallway towards the cargo hold. Jenidayah is talking to Zander and cuts the conversation short when she sees Yukev. She begins to yell at him over the whining din of the engines.

"What the hell is he doing now?"

Tiller tries to explain, "We just got the next set coordinates, and it's in the trench."

"Dreader?"

"Yep."

"This ship can't take Dreader!"

"I—"

"We're going to be crushed like a can!"

"Jenidayah, would you hold on for a—"

The woman unstraps herself from the harness and begins to rise when Zander grabs her arm softly. "Now hold on, miss. Let da man speak. Seems he still got sumfin' tuh say."

Yukev continues, "I told him. He knows. We're only going down a hundred meters and shadowing. But he wants everyone to suit up and make sure they are working."

Zander seems a bit nervous and is staring at the wall with his hands clasped together. He is shaking, and Jenidayah looks over at him and questions, "What's wrong with you?"

Zander's eyes look like they will bulge out of his head. "I-I can't swim. I's gonna drown down deh."

Yukev begins checking some numbers on a wall panel and notices Zander's stare. He looks at Jenidayah and asks, "What's wrong with him?"

She replies, "He's freaked because he can't swim."

The tech replies nonchalantly, "You can go stay in the evac-pods if you feel more comfortable. But if they find us, they're gonna kill you anyway."

Jenidayah and Zander both stare at Yukev and bow their heads.

Yukev questions, "What? Too dramatic? I was actually trying to be funny."

The two shout in unison, "Not funny!"

Jenidayah pulls a suit from the storage locker, quickly sheds her clothes and stands naked in front of them revealing a svelte but well built frame. The men stop talking and quickly turn away while she slips into the suit and starts to put her helmet on. Yukev turns back around and cautions, "I'd wait on the hat for a minute. The suits only have so much air. So top off your tanks and strap in."

The mercenary glares at Tiller, then walks over and quickly attaches a nozzle from a hose on the wall into her suit. She pulls a lever down and watches the gauge of an instrument panel on her wrist. After a moment, the dial is green. Zander suits-up awkwardly then sits down quickly.

Jenidayah grabs Zander's arm firmly and states, "You're in an environmental suit, and we have waterproof escape pods. They'll shoot us long before we drown." She pats his chest and stares at him with a big smile. "Okay?"

The pilot's voice barks through the speaker, "Tiller, we're getting close. What's the status?"

Tiller looks up at the numbers and punches a button to engage the mic. "Once I program the nano-paint to act as a sealer, that's it for the camouflage. They're all gonna know this is the stolen referee ship."

Luval answers, "Copy. Do it. It doesn't matter now anyway."

Yukev acknowledges, "Okay," and begins typing on a tablet he's brought down from the flight deck with him. He stops, looks at Zander, and reassures him, "Don't worry, buddy. It's gonna be fine. Tell ya what. When it's time, we're gonna need you at the gunner's post again, so get ready to do some more shootin', okay? And that stew was great!"

Zander begins to smile and looks at Jenidayah and says, "I likes to shoot. How 'bouts you, little lady? You wanna help me shoot?"

Jenidayah pats him on the back and replies, "Yeah, let's shoot bad guys."

Tiller smiles, hurries back to the front of the ship and up the ladder into the cockpit. He wraps the harness around him and looks over at Tosin. The pilot pushes the yoke forward, and the ship begins a steep dive toward the water. The craft slices through the waves at a sharp angle and then levels off at one hundred meters.

Yukev advises, "Keep the speed down so the nano-wrap doesn't get too much friction."

The pilot nods and pulls back the throttle, and the engines lower from a whine to a throbbing hum.

Tosin and Yukev gaze out the cockpit and marvel at the aquatic world around them. The view is utterly breathtaking, and if it weren't for the severity of their circumstances and the inherent peril of this planet, it would be worthy of a tour with the family. Giant kelp beds reach up from the deep like leafy underwater skyscrapers spanning several hundreds—possibly thousands—of meters from the depths below, with teams of life swimming through the underwater vegetation. Several sea animals attempt to follow along the side of their ship but are no match for the speed of the shuttle.

The pilot queries, "How far?"

"Not much more, but it's several kilometers down," replies the navigator.

Tosin comments, "This is a suicide run. Those other shuttles can't reach that depth either. They're just trying to kill them all."

Yukev counters, "No, we could've done it if we didn't take that hull damage in the jungle. I know the ball can take it. It was made for this stuff."

"So how many ships are left anyway? I lost count."

Yukev keys in a command, and the holographic map displays the remaining ships and their depth with the number of each ship on top of it. "Looks like four," he adds.

The number eight craft, which still has the ball after the Lore Jungle imbroglio, is almost at depth. Inside, the pilot and navigator confer.

"What's our depth?"

"Eight kilos."

"How much longer? This ship isn't going to take too much more of this."

"The bottom is nine point six kilometers. The rules say we only have to hit nine at these coordinates."

"Where are the other ships?"

"They're following, but nobody wants to fire down here because of shockwaves, so we're probably safe until we start to surface."

"Okay, let's get this done and climb out of here."

The navigator nods as the bulkheads of their craft whine and creak in complaint of the enormous pressure they are experiencing.

Tosin and Yukev observe three of the ships dip to the correct depth and begin their upward ascent. As the number one ship, which sustained damage in the faceoff with the number eight craft in the Lore Jungle, reaches the perigee, it blinks and is gone.

"Oh! Almost … but no. Okay the number one ship is toast, and on it's way to a watery grave," comments Tiller, as if he is a sports announcer.

Tosin adds, "Only three to go."

Tiller notices an update on the Nav-Com and advises his pilot, "Looks like we've got new coordinates."

"Man … this can't go on much longer. There's only a couple of hours left before that thing goes off," complains Luval.

The navigator confirms, "Yeah, this is it! The home stretch. It's a mad dash across the Leydan Desert and then a climb into the *Rusage Mountains.* Looks like that's where the nulling ring is."

"Okay, time to get dry."

"No wait! Don't surface yet. There's gonna be referee shuttles and drones all over those three ships. Let them move on, and I'll plot us a shortcut."

Suddenly, a crackling comes over the speaker. "Luval! Get that pasty little geek down here. We got problems!"

Yukev undoes his harness, leaps out of the seat, then slides down the ladder. He races back to the cargo hold and sees both Jenidayah and Zander trying to stop water from streaming through a breach in the hull. The tech pushes the button of a com unit on the wall and barks, "Hey, remember when I said stay underwater?"

The major answers, "Yeah."

"We got a leak. Get outta the water. Now! But don't fly any higher than twenty meters so we stay off their sensors, okay?"

"Understood."

The three crewmembers can feel the ship angle upward and brace themselves. Tiller taps some numbers, and the nano-paint on the outside of the ship turns invisible again. He runs toward the two who are still holding the steel plate as water sprays out the sides. He directs both of them to look away as he ignites a torch and quickly seals the leak. All three sit down on a bench against the side of the bulkhead and catch their breath. Jenidayah warns, "This ship is falling apart! When is this damn game going to end?"

Yukev slows his breathing, turns to the woman warrior, and informs her, "We just got the last set of coordinates."

"Where now?" she quizzes.

"A shortcut across Leydan, and it ends in a pass in Rusage."

"Oh great. A real fire and ice ending," she surmises.

Tiller gets up, sloshes through the water to the back of the ship, and dryly cautions, "Hold on."

He pounds on a large red knob by the back door, and the rear ramp opens with a howl of wind. Tiller grabs a handrail and pulls up his feet as the water drains out of the rear cargo hold. He then hits the knob again, and the ramp door slams shut. Zander and Jenidayah, who quickly had to hold on for dear life, stare at him silently as he walks by. He stops, looks at the woman, then comments, "What? I needed to get rid of the water."

She starts to open her mouth but then raises her hand and bows and shakes her head. "Just … go."

Zander chuckles. "Damn, boy. You crazy!"

Tiller heads back up to the flight deck and plops back down in his seat. He turns to Tosin and adjures, "Why did we bring her again? She's becoming a pain in the ass!"

The pilot smiles and responds, "You haven't seen her fight yet. If we have visitors, you're going to be glad she's here. Plus she can hit a bug at five hundred meters."

Tiller shakes his head. "I dunno, man. She hates you more than Cholash did. Poor guy. I was starting to like him."

The guardsman turns and looks at Yukev. "I feel bad too. He gave his life for us after I beat the crap out of him. This whole thing is a mess."

There are voices in the High Council that feel Drothamae has grown too commercial, barbaric, and embarrassing. Many stories have been told about what happens once the prisoners are released. A classic example is what recently occurred several months back.

Vjorek was now a free man. The video showing the final moments of his spectacular win were still being broadcast throughout the solar system. The convicted murderer but skilled pilot, having his sentence commuted for championing the perilous contest, is back on Seltuvay. He, along with his crew of malcontents, is living it up at a bar where he has celebrity status. Unfortunately, winning the game won his freedom but not any money. So the stocky man with piercings and tattoos throughout his face and body, including a tattoo covering his entire bald head, speaks loudly into a communication device to his old employer over the blaring music in the saloon.

"Dax! Dax, can you hear me?"

A voice comes back through the little speaker. "Barely. Get somewhere quiet."

The burly man rises, knocking over a glass that spills all over the table and floor as his buddies laugh. He yells at his friends, "Aye, get another round. I gotta talk to Dax."

One of the other thugs barks, "Is that Dax? Hey, tell him we're ready to go."

"Shut up!" He walks out of the establishment and into the cool night air before continuing, "Mr. Dax, we need work. They drained our accounts."

"Not possible. You're too hot. You're just out of prison."

"I got a lead on a job. All we need are some new IDs and a ship. It's a sweet take. A shipment of Gelamine on its way to Kree for boss Takahata. We get the goods, and you get to screw over your biggest competitor."

"I don't need it."

"Aw c'mon, Dax. I'd say you owe us, mate."

"Oh? Why is that?"

"Five years on that rock and we never gave you up."

"Mmmm. There is something to be said for loyalty. Contact a man named Loran in Dueshay."

"Now that's more like it. But how do we get there? That's in the southern hemisphere."

"I will send a ground shuttle to your coordinates in an hour. Be ready to go. And, Vjorek?"

"Yeah, mate?"

"Once you do the job, we're even. Keep the shipment. This call never happened. Dax out."

The man lumbers back inside and plops down in a chair at the table with his motley crew.

One of the other men, with long black hair and a scar across his face, named Heldren, queries, "Well?"

Vjorek pauses for a moment, then raises his glass and blurts out, "We're on, boys! Time to get the band back together aye?"

The former convicts all cheer and toast one another forcefully as froth from their glasses spills out onto the table and floor.

The surly man advises, "Okay, he's sending a shuttle to get us. We gotta meet some guy in Dueshay."

"That's on the other side of the damn planet," complains Heldren.

"Yeah, but he told us we could keep the prize. He doesn't want any of it."

"How the hell did you get him to do that?"

"Told him we kept our mouths shut."

The other hoodlums all agree. "Yeah. That's right. Kept our mouths shut we did."

"Okay, one more, and we're done. We need to sober up and go over the job. We won't have much time. When's the shipment supposed to arrive?"

Heldren informs, "Twelve hundred *Kree* time. So we'll need two hours to get from Seltuvay to the moon."

Vjorek downs the glass of foaming liquid and belches loudly before commanding, "Okay, boys, drink up and let's go get rich."

Maytor Dax sits at his desk and stares at a computer screen in front of him. He keys in some digits on the keyboard and sees the face of an aging man with deep ridges in his face, narrow eyes, long gray hair that hangs down and some that is carefully arranged in a bun. The man speaks with a dismissive tone. "Dax. I am surprised by this call. What can I do for you?"

"Boss Takahata. Good to see you are well."

"Get on with it, Maytor. I don—"

"I have some information you might be interested in."

"Oh?"

"It seems someone might try to hijack one of your shipments."

"Maytor, like you, I have several shipments a day throughout the solar system."

"Yes, but not all of them are Gelamine."

"I'm still listening."

"I am willing to give you a gift if it will keep the peace between us."

"Peace? You have been murdering my people for years, Dax. I—"

"Takahata-San, the Libertarium is responsible for a great deal of both our losses. Let's move forward, shall we? After this ... situation is handled, let us sit for a parlay. You can select the location. I will arrive with only one man."

"Maytor, I trust you about as far as I can throw a space cruiser, but … I am intrigued."

"I will send you the information I have, and may I recommend that you alter your shipment schedule. Once the hijackers have been dealt with, we can set up a meeting."

"Agreed."

"I am forwarding the particulars now."

The white-haired man views the images, and his already narrow eyes squint into a set of slits as he looks at Dax. "I don't trust you, Dax. But if this is true, you have saved me several million credits."

"My pleasure, Boss Takahata. Please let me know how things turn out, and we'll get together sometime next week. Sound good?"

"Next week. Takahata out."

The fat crime lord finishes a meal he had been enjoying before this issue started and thinks to himself, *Two birds with one stone … excellent.*

A hooded man greets the gang members as they enter an abandoned warehouse after a long ride from the northern hemisphere in a ground shuttle. The large bald man asks, "Are you Loran? I'm Vj—"

"Yes, Vjorek. Distinguished winner of the latest round of Drothamae. And I suppose this is your crew." Loran points to the other three criminals.

"Yeah, at's right, mate."

"Maytor Dax sends his congratulations on your win. As a gesture of good will for you past service to his company, he bestows you with this gift." The man hits a key on a wrist device, and the building lights up to reveal a matte-black ship with government markings parked behind him.

Vjorek begins to walk around the craft while the hooded man

continues, "This is an older model, but it is fully functional and configured for orbital and space travel. Unfortunately, we had very short notice, so while it is fueled, we weren't able to arm it as well as we'd liked."

The large criminal pilot questions, "What's it got?"

"Three pulse cannons—fore, aft, and underneath, which are fully charged, but only two missiles with conventional loads. No Nukes. No drones. No mines."

"Tactical arms?" queries Heldren.

"Four laser rifles. Ten stun grenades. Three particle bombs—medium yield. As I mentioned, we had very little time."

The crew looks at each other as the pilot continues walking around the military craft, running his hands across the smooth steel plates of the armor and then inspecting the triangular openings of the large engine pods on top of the stubby wings.

"It's fine. What the hell … it's free!"

The hooded man bows and retreats into the darkness with parting words. "Maytor Dax wishes you good hunting but asks that you never contact him again. I bid you all adieu, gentlemen." He disappears out the door and can be heard giving orders to a group of men outside the makeshift hangar. Several vehicles all power up and leave the area with a crack from their beam drives—which power most ground transportation in this solar system.

Vjorek orders, "Okay, boys, let's get to work. I wanna be airborne in thirty minutes," before turning and jogging up the cargo ramp at the back of the spacecraft.

He turns back towards Heldren and cautions, "Sweep the ship for bugs and bombs, mate!"

The longhair, while typing quickly on a tablet, nods without lifting his head. The other two men, twin brothers with platinum-white short hair and matching tattoos but on opposite sides of their faces, gather up the weapons lying on the floor and begin stowing them in the cargo hold.

Vjorek is going over the instrumentation and doing a preflight check when Heldren climbs up the ladder and drops a handful of devices on the floor of the flight deck. The pilot turns and views the pile as the thin and lanky longhair confirms his suspicions. "Well … you were right. I'm pretty sure that's all the bugs."

"Any other surprises?"

"Two particle bombs stowed near the engines. Maximum yield."

"I knew it was too easy."

"Dax probably ratted us out to Takahata too," adds the navigator.

"Mmmm. See if you can get in touch with our friends. Maybe we can still salvage this run. What did you do with the bombs?"

"I deactivated the remote detonators. They're outside on the floor."

"Can you rig them as gravity bombs?"

"Yeah sure. What for?"

"We've only got two missiles. They might come in handy."

"Okay, man, but I'll need a couple more minutes."

"Negative … we need to get in the air, mate."

"No way!" complains Heldren. "Too sensitive. I need to do this on the ground or … *boom*." He imitates an explosion with his hands.

Vjorek acquiesces. "Okay, you're the bomb tech. But hurry!"

Heldren makes the explosion motion with his hands again before shaking his head and climbing down the ladder of the flight deck.

Within half an hour, the ship is airborne and heading for Kree. Heldren is fidgeting in the copilot's chair with a small vial of purplish goo. He dips a straw into the little bottle and snorts a long draw into his hawkish nose. He recoils back into the seat and begins to convulse and tremble as the effects of the highly addictive drug begin to course through his body. The pilot shouts in an irritated tone, "Aye! What the hell!"

The copilot pants several times before answering, "I-I just needed a little … whew … a little bump, man. We've been up for twenty hours."

The pilot says disgustedly, "If you blow this, I'll give you a *bump!* I will end you myself. Any word from our associates?"

Heldren, now slightly slurring his words, replies, "They're going through with the shipment anyway. They just changed the location to a deserted island chain." The navigator keys in some commands, and a holographic image of the moon appears. There is a pulsing red circle around the new rendezvous location in the southern hemisphere.

The pilot queries his navigator, "Okay, can you set this ship for remote control?"

"Uh yeah. Why?"

"I wanna get to that island, offload our weapons, and then send the ship back toward Silion as bait. Once Takahata thinks he's destroyed Dax's ship, we ambush them and steal theirs."

Heldren thinks for a moment then answers, "It could work. I'll need to sweep Takahata's ship for countermeasures too. And we won't have much time."

"Do you have time to rig a jammer?"

"Probably. How long before we enter Kree's orbit?"

Vjorek looks at his instrumentation. "Hour and a half."

Heldren requests "Back off the throttle a bit. Your instruments might go a little screwy while I'm … securing some parts."

"Long as the ship don't quit running, I'm good, mate."

Heldren cracks his neck from side to side then tries to shake off the effects of the Gelamine before mentioning, "I need to go down to the cargo hold for this." The longhair begins ripping modules out of the wall and collecting the parts under one arm before climbing back down the ladder.

As the craft nears Kree, Vjorek radios back to his navigator, "Hey, brotha, how's it comin' back there?"

A voice crackles back through the speaker. "Good. Nearly done. Once I fire this up though, you're going to have to fly line of sight. You're instruments will be useless. Okay?"

"Roger that," the pilot acknowledges.

"Okay, jamming commencing in three, two, one. Jammed!"

Alarms go off in the cockpit, and several of the instruments begin to blink wildly. The heads-up display on the front windshield vanishes. The pilot feels the steering become more sluggish just as Heldren climbs back up and drops into the copilot's chair.

"Hell! It's like driving a container carrier," complains the pilot.

"Yeah, these shuttles use navigation assistance on the flight controls. She's probably not happy about this."

Vjorek returns, "Well then best we not tell her about the next part of the plan … aye, mate? Think you can get us some bearings on that fancy little gadget of yours?"

Heldren smiles as he keys in some commands on his tablet then answers, "I'm linking navigation to my computer. This should smooth things out."

A smaller holographic map appears with a line marking their trajectory to a deserted island on the southern hemisphere of the moon.

Heldren advises, "Once we de-orbit, fly just under fifty meters, and we'll be below sensors. Just hug the water all the way to the island and bank around the north end. There's a beach there that we can offload the gear to. After that, I'll take over control of the ship, bring it up to suborbital flight, and disengage the jammer. It'll light up like a sign. They will track it all the way to Silion."

The pilot follows his navigator's directions, landing the ship on the deserted beach. Vjorek and the two criminal brothers quickly remove the weapons and several other large cases from the cargo hold. Heldren punches in some code on a keypad as he pretends to talk to the ship, "Sorry, baby. Wish we had more time together, but I gotta go and I need you to do me one last favor, honey. Okay?" He keys in two more commands on his tablet, and a readout confirms that the ship is now under remote control. He stands and pats the side of the bulkhead before climbing down the ladder and then trotting briskly through the cargo hold and down the exit ramp. He joins his fellow gang members and looks at Vjorek. He confirms, "We're good to go. Too bad. I was kinda getting used to her." He turns and gazes at the shuttle in the sunlight.

Vjorek looks at a wrist device and checks the time, then directs Heldren, "Time to send your new girlfriend away."

The longhaired man swipes at his tablet, and the craft lifts off and streaks north toward the original rendezvous point.

Heldren turns to the large crook and informs, "Okay, it's on autopilot, but now that I have disengaged the jammer, it won't be long before they see it coming."

Vjorek commands, "C'mon, men, we gotta move."

The four men hike inland from the beach then use machetes to hack a path through the thick brush. They reach the other side of the island and squat behind some trees, spying a space transport with calligraphy on the sides of it confirming it belongs to boss Takahata. Two gangsters are carrying crates off the spacecraft and stowing them into the nearby ground shuttle.

The bald pilot whispers, "Okay, men, we won't have much time for this smash and grab. Try to concentrate your fire away from the transport. We need that ship. Got it?"

The other three nod while preparing their weapons. Heldren has the modified particle bombs in a satchel slung over his shoulder. Vjorek puts his hand on his longhaired friend and reminds him, "Wait until we're in the air before you use them, okay?"

Heldren responds with a quick wink and a smile, then softly utters, "Boom!"

The freed felons burst out of the bushes and begin blazing away at Takahata's men. Two are cut down immediately, and another two retreat behind the hovercraft. A pilot inside the orbital transport begins powering up the engines, but the twins make a dash, managing to get up the ramp of the ship before it starts to close. As the craft lifts off, flashes of light can be seen through the large windshield of the cockpit, and it lurches and plops back down, sending a cloud of dust and sand everywhere. Four other men come out of a thicket on the other side of the clearing, but the twins, now in the shuttle, train its pulse cannons and annihilate them with a withering stream of blue energy. The two Takahata men sill trapped behind the ground shuttle hop in it and attempt a get away, but Heldren manages to lob one of the particle bombs at the fleeing craft, and within seconds it is blown to bits, sending a pressure wave back that knocks both the longhair and his bald pilot to the ground.

The twins rush down the ramp out of the ship, kneel next to Vjorek and Heldren, and begin shaking the unconscious crooks. After a moment, the pilot and tech awaken with Vjorek lambasting his cohort. "What the hell! Heldren! What did I tell you about those damn bombs!"

The tech shakes the sand out his hair and replies, "Did you want them to get away?"

The pilot stares at him and admits, "Well, no, but …"

"Well, all right then. It's done." He rises to his feet and extends an arm to the burly man.

One of the twins comments, "We might have a problem in the cockpit."

Heldren snipes, "What did you do!"

The other blond twin admits, "He was gonna get away. We had to do something."

The four of them run into the ship and climb up the ladder to the flight deck. There is still a small fire, and Heldren quickly grabs a fire suppressor off the wall and extinguishes it. Vjorek stares at the dead pilot still in the chair and yells in disgust, "So you shot up the damn cockpit?" He lifts the pilot up with one arm, showing his great strength, and flings the body, which clears the deck and lands in the cargo hold below with a thud. He turns to the twins and commands, "Get him off the ship," then turns his attention to the tech. "Heldren?"

The thin man pulls his long black hair back into a ponytail, then pauses for a long moment, surveying the damage before replying, "I'm not sure. They did a number on it. I need some time."

"What about the other ship?"

"Most likely almost at the coordinates." He looks down at his tablet.

"Can you turn it around?"

"Yeah, but there'll be an armada following it by the time it gets here, between Takahata's men and the System Guard."

"Okay, I'm going to see what's left of the shipment. See what you can do. But we can't stay here long or we'll be—"

Suddenly a blast hits Vjorek in the side of the head, opening up most of his skull against the front windshield. The next pulse hits Heldren square in the gut and separates the top and bottom of his body into two bloody parts. The hooded man, who had been hiding in a compartment of the cargo hold before climbing up to the flight deck, turns and trains the large-caliber pulse weapon at the twins on the lower deck. He cuts them down while still standing on the ladder, then climbs back up into the bloodied cockpit and grabs the tablet from the hand of the severed tech's body. He keys in some commands and watches a video feed from the rogue ship's front camera that shows the craft dive straight into a building that houses Takahata's main operations.

Loran pulls his hood back and contacts his employer. "This is Loran."

A voice crackles back through the speaker. "And?"

"It's done."

"What about Takahata?"

"The complex is destroyed. But we will need to wait for forensics to confirm the outcome."

"Get the Gelamine. Dax out."

MERCENARIES TO THE RESCUE

aytor Dax invested large sums for mercenaries to track down the Libertarium, only to have the men he dispatched returned to him either; burnt beyond recognition or in pieces. A scourge on the scourge, and it's only getting worse. The *Daxian Resolve* was probably the best thing to happen to the cartel because he was starting to loose a lot of men, and the financial impact to his criminal enterprise has been astounding. He fears he is losing control, and realizes something needs to be done but is in a quandary on how to proceed against such a shadowy force.

Libertarium recon had verified the Daxian Cartel's location in the Gureeg Asteroid Belt, and Na'edra then approved the rescue mission.

The cabin of the small attack ship is dark except for a dim red hue from the emergency lighting and the reflection of the readouts dancing on the displays in front of the pilot and navigator.

The pilot communicates via radio to the soldiers in the rear cargo hold, "We will reach the edge of their radar soon. At that point, we go quiet, and you will exit the rear of the craft on your sleds. Make sure all your electronics are in safe mode. If not, you'll light up like a sign, and they'll pick you off like fish in a barrel."

The voice of Captain Godan back in the cargo hold crackles through the speaker and acknowledges, "Copy."

A light turns green on the side of the cargo hold, and the air is quickly purged from the compartment with a loud hiss. Once the hold is depressurized, a ramp door is opened in the rear of the craft, and the soldiers, now lying on rocket sleds begin to exit the craft into space. Deep blue flames ignite from the sleek tactical vehicles and they arrange into a triangle formation in front of the craft before disappearing into the cold, dark cosmos.

The pilot radios back to Libertarium command, "Operation Freedom Flight is now underway."

Na'edra leans over a communications station on Ultan and acknowledges, "Copy. Please initiate radio silence and let's pray for our men."

The pilot responds, "Will re-establish contact when the package has been received. Going dark."

He presses several buttons, and the ship becomes unidentifiable amidst the blackness surrounding it.

The mercenary leader checks the configuration of his men behind him. He is flying point on the tactical sleds. The small squad is now coasting after the initial burn from their engines. The element of surprise is key to their mission. While the sleds are too small to be seen on long-distance scanners, they still possess radar-deflecting coverings. The asteroid, almost the size of a small moon, grows larger as they approach. The attack force is using a scrambled encryption algorithm—which sounds like background radiation without the proper decryption cypher—and the commander cautions his men, "Okay, everyone stay tight and alert. No chatter. We should reach the surface in fifteen minutes. Remember the plan."

The group responds in unison, "Copy."

Dax's bloated belly bounces up and down as he waddles into a holding cell where Desiree and her child are being kept. The metal door slams shut behind him, and stares at her intensely before threatening, "While I want to dispose of you and your little pup right now, I'm waiting. Once you witness the death of your piece of crap husband, I will kill both of you." He turns a video screen on that shows the game being broadcast before adding, "It won't be long now." As he strokes the side of her face, Desiree bites deep into a fleshy part of his arm, then spits the ripped skin back into his face.

He yowls in pain and smashes a fist into her head. "You bitch!"

He holds the wound with his other hand, then screams, "Guard! Get me out of here!"

The door opens, and he hurries out of the room. Once he is gone, Robey leaps up and rips a piece of his shirt off and wipes the blood from his mother's forehead and mouth. She hugs him and sobs, "Oh, my sweet boy. I'm so sorry. If only he were here."

Robey remarks, "Don't worry, Mom. I've got a feeling. I dunno how or why, but … I think we're going to be okay."

Desiree gazes at her son affectionately and forces a smile as she caresses the side of his face. "Let's hope so," as they stare at the images of the shuttles on the screen.

Maytor Dax, now with his left hand bandaged, paces back and forth in front of bank of monitors and barks, "Anything?"

A man sitting at the monitoring station replies, "No, sir. After the Dreader Trench, they broadcast the final coordinates for the Rusage Mountains, but there's been no sign of Luval. They're still checking the jungle, and they think a Kragor ate him and the crew. They're trying to find the beast to cut it open."

The fat man ponders for a moment, still nursing the deep bite from Desiree. He turns to leave, then stops and orders, "I want to know the moment they have the beast."

The subordinate responds, "Yes, sir."

The mercenary force lands several kilometers from Dax's complex. With almost no gravity, it is easy for the squad, who has trained for missions like these, to take giant leaps and cover great distances. They reach the edge of the underground compound in a short amount of time, and elect to enter by way of a small maintenance door. Marked only by a small kiosk that protrudes up out of the craggy rock surface, the team surveys the area before moving in. One of the mercenaries sets up a jamming device and switches it on. A sequence of lights turns from red to green. He looks up at his commander and gives him a gloved thumbs-up sign. Two other members of the squad slither over to the door and slap a device on the lock. One presses a button on a control bracelet on his arm, and a sonic charge blasts the lock open. A crook stationed inside the airlock is caught off guard and killed before he has time to warn of the intrusion, while the rest of the team quickly enters and re-pressurizes the airlock.

One of Dax's men in the control room notices a small glitch in the cameras before they return to normal. He begins contacting all the guards at different points of the base. "This is master control. All posts sound off. Have you noticed anything?" Replies start to crackle in over the speaker.

"This is hangar bay. Everything's normal here."

"Detention … all quiet down here, except the wife is crying."

"Armory here. We got nothin'."

"Main gate is nominal. Why?"

The thug in the control room waits for a second, then radios again. "Maintenance. What's your status?"

Captain Godan nods to one of his team, who has taken the com unit from the dead gang member and begins talking while scratching at the device.

"Every th- fi- ere. No pro—"

The control officer repeats, "Maintenance, what was that? You are breaking up."

There is another garbled response.

"I - noth - t - rep—"

The control officer, frustrated with the reply, orders the guard, "Your com unit is failing. Take it to tech once you're off your shift!"

The mercenary answers while pressing the on-off button, "Cop-will d- out."

The hoodlum looks back at the displays, spying for any anomalies, and then shakes his head and goes back to watching the readouts and commentary about the ongoing game of Death Ball.

The mercenaries move briskly down the hallways toward the holding cells. They stop before turning the last corner and use a small snaking camera to survey the jail. The image displayed on their visors reveals two henchmen guarding a door. Godan motions orders with his hands. Two of the soldiers roll little balls around the corner that speed up and stop at the thugs' feet. They look down at the shiny spheres, which suddenly emit a blinding white light, rendering them unconscious without making any noise. They fall to the floor, and the rescue squad quickly moves to the door. Captain Godan pulls up his visor and speaks through the small square portal in the steel door, "Ma'am, I need you to move to the back of the cell please."

Desiree Luval replies, "Oh thank goodness! Are you System Guard?"

Godan answers, "Uh no. Not anymore. There's no time. Please stand back!"

The woman grabs her son, and they move to the back of the cell, and tilt the cot in front of them. Another member places a sonic charge on the lock and blows it, but it doesn't unlock. He looks at his commander and shakes his head. "Didn't work, sir."

Godan orders, "Plastic. Now!"

The soldier reaches in a bag and pulls out two clumps of a putty-like substance and applies it on the hinges. The rest of the force retreats from the door, and he gives the order. The munitions officer keys a command on his arm bracelet, and the goop explodes. The door falls outward and slams onto the concrete floor. Three members run in and grab the woman and child and bring them out into the hallway. Godan comments dryly, "So much for secrecy. Let's move like we have a purpose, gentlemen."

One of the other team members pulls some clothes out of a bag and gives them to Desiree. "Ma'am, I need you and your son to put these on quickly."

Desiree recognizes the material and acknowledges, "Robey, sweetie, we need to put these environment suits on. Okay, baby. Quickly!"

The boy hops into the one-piece suit and is actually finished before his mother. The squad surrounds them, and all jog the hallway toward the hangar bay.

Commander Godan radios his ship, "We have the package. Begin countermeasures. We're heading to the hangar bay now. Suspect LZ will be hot."

"Copy. Commencing countermeasures now. Stay low because it's gonna be hellfire for a minute or two."

The commander turns to the team and advises, "Let's get back out through the maintenance shaft. They need to clear the bay before dust off."

As they turn, two of Dax's men begin firing laser rifles in a hail of searing red blasts. One of the team member's arms falls to the ground as the light slices through his shoulder, and he shrieks in pain. Godan fixes his weapon on the assailant and blows him apart with two blasts. The other thug retreats, and three of the squad members chase after him while a medic tends to the fallen soldier.

"Get him stable! We need to go now!" advises the commander.

The medic applies foam that quickly solidifies around the wound, and he and another soldier lift the man as they proceed back down the corridor the way they came. Additional laser fire can be heard in front of them, and they cautiously go around a turn to find their fellow men with a pile of bodies on the floor. They regroup and continue up a set of stairs. Dust suddenly begins to fall from the ceiling, and the building shakes from the bombardment now taking place from orbit as the Libertarium spacecraft begins pounding the facility at will.

Maytor Dax stumbles over himself into the control room and

chortles, "What the hell is going on! Get Clog on the line! The System Guard will pay for this!"

The man at the displays returns, "It's not the guard."

"Well who is it!"

"I think it's the Libertarium, sir."

"Libertarium! What the hell do they want? Wait … that's it. They're working with Luval. Return fire!"

"We can't, sir. They destroyed most of our defenses!"

"Get the whore and her brat! We're getting out of here."

Another henchmen rushes into the room and shouts over the din of destruction, "They took them, sir. They're gone!"

Dax spins out of the room, trundles down a hallway to a door several meters away, and punches in a code on a keypad. The door slides open to reveal a Quantum Matter Shifting Pod. He hops into the large device, barely fitting in it because of his extremely wide girth, and slides the top over the opening quickly. Pieces of ceiling are falling all around him as he activates the machine. An intense blue light emanates out of the window of the capsule. Suddenly a huge chunk of concrete comes down and crushes the pod causing it to explode.

The view through the front window of the shuttle reveals a vast barren sea of sand and dunes stretching out to the horizon. The navigator plotted a course across the Leydan desert because it would cut half the time of reaching the final location of the nulling ring. The trek was uneventful, and Yukev returns to the flight deck while still talking in his com. He ends the call with a final remark. "Okay, roger that. He'll be happy to hear. Out." He turns to the pilot and grins widely. "They got her."

"Robey! What about Robey?" the pilot demands.

"Safe. They're both safe, healthy, and on board a Libertarium cruiser on its way back to Ultan," assures the navigator.

Tosin bows his head and heaves an enormous sigh. Suddenly a warning starts beeping in the cockpit, and the ship heaves violently. Tiller barks, "We got company!"

The pilot orders over the com, "Jen, Zander! Man the guns. Looks like they found us."

In the rear hold, they scramble to seats with gunner's yokes in them. Jenidayah is already firing before she has even sat down, and they lay down a punishing stream of light at the pursuing ship. A pulse rocks their ship, and it begins to dive. The woman unloads another salvo, and the image of the ship in her screen explodes into a massive fireball. Tosin's voice comes over the speaker. "Brace for impact! We're going down!"

The pilot fights for control of the craft and is able to level it off, but it's too late. The shuttle clips the edge of a high sand dune, and after two more hops, the ship grinds to a stop by a rocky outcropping that indicates they are near the end of the vast desert.

The craft lie motionless as dust from the crash-landing begins to settle. The guard ship in the distance is engulfed in flames after having exploded. The impact detonated its entire ordinance into an enormous fireball. The wailing alarms in the cockpit help to awaken Tosin from unconsciousness. Yukev is slouched forward with a small streak of blood running down the side of his head. Tosin quickly unbuckles himself, reaches over, and gently touches the thin navigator's neck. His pulse is strong. Tiller's eyes open, and he pulls away from Luval quickly. "Aye, what are you doing?"

The pilot replies, "Yukev, relax. I was just checking if you were still alive."

"Of course I'm alive. What happened?"

"Well, we were ambushed by a guard ship and—"

"No, not that part! I know that. I just can't remember anything after that."

"Your harness came undone while I hit the air brakes, and you took a pretty bad knock to your head."

Yukev puts his hand up to the side of his head and realizes he's bleeding. He jumps out of his flight seat and complains, "I hate blood. Especially mine! I'm gonna go find a med kit."

Tosin requests, "Hey, check on the others. Okay?"

Yukev moves a piece of metal out of the way and calls out as he climbs down off the flight deck, "We're gonna need to do something. There's gonna be more of them soon."

Tosin says, "I know," while he clicks buttons and switches, surveying the damage. "I'm going to need you back up here to get th—"

"Yeah yeah yeah, to get the ship running. Just … just give me a damn minute. Augh! My head is killing me." He plods back onto the cargo deck.

He can hear Jenidayah Horn yelling, "I have had it with that guy. He's going get us killed!" She unbuckles her harness and stands, then kicks a piece of fallen debris, which slams against the opposite bulkhead.

Zander shouts back, "Yo! Hold on now. Don't be hollin' at me, young lady. I'm back here witch yo ass. Y'all got a problem, talk to duh pilot. Leave my ass out of it."

The tall woman glares at Yukev, who is administering a gel to the wound on his head, and demands, "Where is that son of a bitch!"

Yukev yelps under his breath from the pain while the gel solidifies on his head. "He's still in the cockpit. Go easy on him. We're lucky to be alive. Honestly, I don't know how he got us out of that flat spin. But then … I wasn't conscious."

She stares at the pasty man and opens her mouth to say something but then closes it and hits the large knob by the ramp. It creaks for a second and then opens slowly down onto sand, like a large animal yawning. A wave of hot air floods the cargo bay.

Yukev complains, "Aww, man? Close that door. We're at the edge of Leydan at noon! It's too damn hot. If you're goin' out there, you're gonna need your suit. She grabs the helmet of the environmental suit off the floor of the cargo hold, covers her head and locks it in place. She then puts a silver heat-shielding cloak on. Jenidayah pulls the hood of the robe over her helmet, then trots down the ramp. Once she is on the sand, Yukev punches the knob for the door control, and the ramp begins to close. He yells at her, "Keep your com on!"

Now with helmet's sun visor masking her face, she gives the navigator a middle-finger gesture before the large ramp slams shut.

Zander looks up at Tiller. "I don't care how fine she is, dat damn girl's mouth givin' me a headache."

"Mmmm, yeah she's a handful. I gotta get back up there." The tech motions toward the flight deck.

"You need help?"

"Nah just do me a favor and try to clean up back here, okay? And check the weapons pods to see what we got left."

Zander smiles with big white teeth and eyes wide against his dark face. "You got it, boss. And tell Tosin thanks for not gettin' us killed." He motions toward the cockpit.

"We ain't outta here yet, so …"

Tiller turns and walks slowly back toward the stairs up to the flight deck while touching the now dried patch over his wound.

Jenidayah spies the sheer and craggy rock wall of the mountain range behind them that drops onto the parched and fractured ground, which resembles cracked, khaki glass. As she peers through her visor to the east, the shattered, hard-baked dirt gives way to a dry and scalding sea of sand that stretches out to the horizon. The Leydan desert is truly the most desolate place on an already deadly planet. The heat on the open sand rises well above any living thing's tolerance. She covers her face and stares up at the orange and red glow of Lothi, as the ringed gas giant beats down radiation from high in the sky. While the environment suit protects her, the scorching air outside brings back memories of her home world—Ultan. Jenidayah clicks a button on the arm controller, and numbers become visible on her visor as she begins surveying the hull for any damage. She hears Tosin Luval's voice in her helmet. "Jen. Are you okay?"

She begins complaining, "I was fine back at that storage facility. I had food. No one around. And I was safe. Damn you!"

The major tries to assuage her rage. "Jen, they would've found you. We're going to expose them. You'll be free!"

"I'll be dead! Just … stop it. Tell the nerd to fix the damn ship and let's get the hell out of here."

Yukev drops a clump of wires he's holding and starts to yell back, "Hey, tell her she can go—"

The pilot cuts him off. "He's working on it. We should be out of here in—"

Tiller shouts, "It's gonna take a w—"

Luval cuts him off with a motion from his hand before answering,

"An hour. Yukev said no more than an hour. Please don't stay out there too long. We have life support restored in here, so it's cool." He quickly turns off the com before his navigator explodes.

"What! Are you nuts? I need at le—"

"We need to get out of here. Get propulsion online. You can fix the nav once we're airborne again."

"Oh—fix propulsion. Just like that. Like it's nothing sp—"

"Yukev! I need you to concentrate. We are dead if I can't get us in the air."

The tech drops the wires and informs, "I gotta go outside. But you … flying with no instruments? That scares me."

"Get us off the ground. I fly. You fix. Got it?"

"Got it," the tech replies sarcastically as he quickly goes back down the stepladder toward the rear of the shuttle. He trots to the rear ramp and notices that Zander has almost finished stowing everything back into the compartments. He looks at the husky man and comments, "Whoa! How'd you get this—"

Zander grins. "I was duh top prison janitor. You knows, I kinda miss it now. Least it was safe. Dis crap is gettin' nuts. Now where's you goin'?"

Tiller replies while putting on a suit, "I need to go outside and check something. We gotta get outta here soon, so I need to do a patch on the engine manifold. I could use your help."

Zander creases his forehead. "I ain't dat good wit machines. Least not ones dat don't fire no bullets."

Yukev assures, "I just need you to hold up the cover of the engine pod so it doesn't fall on my head."

"Oh, dat different. You bet, boss. I's gonna take dis suit off but guessin' I'm good ta go."

While Jenidayah is walking around the outside of the craft surveying for damage, a man jumps up from behind her and grabs at her suit's environment pack, trying to pull the hoses apart. She dodges his advance and throws a front kick that lands squarely in the helmeted man's chest, knocking him down into the sand. The aggressor aims a pulse weapon at her and unloads several blasts, but she somersaults out of the way and hides behind the stubby wing of the ship. Tosin can hear the commotion and radios her. "Jen! What's going on? I heard laser fire. Are you okay?"

"Looks like there was a survivor from that ship. I don't think they're guardsmen though." She dodges more energy streams being trained on her.

The pilot petitions, "Yukev. Zander! Get out there and help her. I have no electronics up here, so I can't use any of the weapons!"

Jenidayah leaps onto the wing and slides across it feet first and then delivers a crushing blow to the assailant, cracking the visor of his helmet. The two exchange punches and kicks in a heated battle. She flips over him, wraps her hands around his helmet, and pulls it off. The searing heat and air begin to affect him but not before he pulls out a knife and starts lunging wildly at Jenidayah. She grabs his arm, frees the knife, and then buries it into his forehead. A stream of blood exits the wound, and he crumbles onto the sand.

Tosin is about to leave the cockpit but contacts her again. "Jen. *Jen!* Are you there? What's going on? Damn it, guys, get out there!"

The warrior woman catches her breath and then answers, "I'm fine. This bastard is a gang member. He's got a Daxian tattoo on his head."

"So he's got men in the force too?"

"Guess so. And I'm sure these aren't the only ones either."

"Did you get hurt?"

"No. But I did use the Takahata move."

"Oh?"

"Yeah … you know … the one you used on me?"

"General Takahata was a great teacher. I have no idea why he would want to turn to crime."

Jenidayah warns, "You better get the nerd out here and get this thing fixed. I'm going to keep looking and make sure there aren't any more of Dax's men snooping around."

"Copy. Tiller! Where the hell are you?"

"We're just leaving the ship now."

The two men trudge down the ramp and slog through the soft sand toward Jenidayah, who is sitting in the sand next to the dead criminal. Yukev inquires into his headset, "So?"

The mercenary pulls up her sun visor and responds, "I didn't have much time because of this." She points to the corpse. "I'm going to do another walk around and make sure we're alone."

Yukev informs, "Onboard systems aren't up yet. I need to get the engines working first."

"Well how the hell are we going to launch?"

"He's gonna do it manually."

"Manual!"

"Look, I wasn't happy about it either, but we gotta get airborne fast. They're gonna be here within the hour."

"I'm really starting to have my doubts about him."

"Yeah, yeah, whatever. Once you think it's clear, get back inside. I won't be long."

Jenidayah nods in approval before she spins and trots out of view. Tiller and Zander traverse the hot ground over to one of the engine ports. After opening a lid and working on the engine for several minutes, he turns and comments to Zander, "Okay, we're good. Let's get back inside before we turn into broiled steaks!"

Zander remarks, "Oh don't say dat. I could use a nice steak right about now."

Tiller closes the lid to the engine port then stops. An alarm goes off in his helmet, and he looks toward Zander. He radios to Tosin, "Do you see any—"

Luval returns, "Tiller, what did you say?"

The tech plods quickly through the sand up onto a dune and

stares south into the sky, then barks, "Drones! Two coming hot from southeast at three o'clock!"

Luval responds, "Nav is down, so I don't have any radar in here."

Tiller complains, "The nano-wrap isn't working. They can see us! Lean over to my console and check the front overhead panel. Do you see a switch that says Targeting Control?

Tosin confirms, "Yeah, I see it."

Yukev appeals to the pilot, "Flip the switch to *Helmet Mode.*"

The pilot dives over the center console and quickly complies with his navigator's request. Outside, Yukev turns toward the upper gun turret and keys in a command on his tablet and arm bracelet control. The turret immediately spins and faces the sky and starts to turn and adjust, matching Yukev's head movements. Images of red boxes around the little unmanned vehicles are displayed on the inside of his helmet visor confirming a target lock. He pushes on the control bracelet, and the cannons unleash a flurry of bright pulses. The blue energy blazes upward and quickly destroys one of the drones. However, the other manages to dodge out of the way and begins to circle around to the north of the craft.

Jenidayah radios to Yukev, "If that gets out of range, we're screwed! They probably already have a fix on us!"

Yukev comments under his breath, "Yeah but not for long."

He keys another command, and a red drone bursts out of the top of the craft and quickly shrinks away into the sky in pursuit. After closing the gap on the evading vehicle, the navigator pounds his finger on the arm bracelet again, and it emits a narrow white beam of light from an onboard laser. The other drone explodes into pieces. Tiller keys in a final command, and the drone flies back and nests itself into the small pod bay in the top of the ship.

The rest of the crew shouts, "Whoa! Nice!"

Yukev answers, "Yeah, we got one of those too."

The two prisoners head back toward the ramp as the wind starts to kick up sand.

Once inside, Yukev takes off his enviro-suit, heads up to the flight deck, and plops down into his seat. He looks over at his pilot while taking off a shoe, then dumps sand out of it.

Luval ignites the thrusters and pulls hard on the yoke. The craft yowls and creaks in complaint as it leaps off the sand and then streaks into the air, sending Tiller back into his seat. Jenidayah comes over the speaker, "Damn it, Luval! What the hell is wrong with you!"

The major answers, "Sorry, Jen. We have to get out of here now."

He turns to Tiller and commands, "Nav—fast!"

Yukev, already holding a bundle of wires with one hand and furiously typing with another, stops momentarily and makes a dismissing motion with his arm before continuing the task. Luval banks hard to port and spins away from the desert in a northwesterly direction. He looks down at the chronometer on his wrist—standard issue to guardsmen and the only other possession besides his glasses he was able to keep after he was incarcerated. The timer reads only four hours left. Suddenly the instrumentation all lights up, and Tiller slumps back in his chair in a moment of exhaustion.

Luval leans over and pats the skinny man on his boney shoulder. "Good job. Tiller. I knew you could do it. Do we have a fix on the ball?"

Yukev glares at the major. "Jeez! Can I have a moment here?"

Tosin replies, "No time. Just get me a fix, and then you can rest."

The navigator shakes his head and then types in some commands. An image of the ball appears on the heads-up display, and Yukev reports, "Okay, we're here. The nulling ring is in the middle of the Rusage Mountains. I mapped out a shortcut that will intersect with the group, but you need to hug the terrain so their sensors don't spot us. Now … I wanna go get some of the sand outta my shorts … mind?"

Luval smiles and nods. "Yeah go ahead. Tell Jen and Zander to be ready. They're probably sending reinforcements for us now."

Yukev complains, "I dunno why. They know where we're going," as he climbs down the ladder.

The High Council has convened a special quorum, and Reital Lieth, the representative from Flon D'Mar addresses the other assembled members. He is a tall man with dark hair and a light complexion, which highlights the weakness of the sun on his home planet. He paces in front of a large video screen on the wall with split images. On the left are the statistics of the ongoing game of Drothamae. Displayed to the right are a number of documents.

Reital begins, "Distinguished sirs and madams, thank you for joining me here today. I know many of you would rather be at home watching Drothamae with your loved ones, but we have matters of a serious nature and the utmost importance to discuss. We all know the unfortunate outcome of the Daxian Resolve campaign, and with the conviction of Tosin Luval, we thought we could put this all behind us. But new information has come to light that casts a shadow on both the evidence presented at the trial and the possibility of complacency, treachery, and the involvement of high-ranking members of this administration."

There are gasps from the members of the council, and Faylen Clog stands and demands, "Where is the proof of this? How *dare* you tarnish the good name of this council with these accusations!"

"Please, please. Calm down. All evidence will be presented for your review in a timely manner," Reital assures his constituents. "But due to the sensitive nature of these findings, we will need to sequester the council." Suddenly all the doors slam shut, and the collected body of politicians gasps in unison.

"What is the meaning of this!" demands Clog.

Reital responds, "Prime Minister, Warden Frukas's father has been assassinated on Seltuvay, and the System Guard has indicated that the only way to protect you all during this turbulent time is to lock down the capital. As such, we will remain here until the end of the game and hash through the findings until we have revealed who the traitor amongst us is."

All the members begin to complain, but Reital holds up his hands and assures them, "The proof is incontrovertible, and there isn't much time left, so please be seated and let us get to business."

Everyone but Clog agrees, and sits while he stares intensely at the Flon representative.. "I will have your head for this," he says before being seated.

Reital adds, "Maybe so, councilman. Maybe so. But let us get started. Shall we?"

Clog waves a hand as if to acquiesce to Reital. The room goes dark, and the section of video screen displaying the contest slides away. It goes full screen and begins displaying images as Reital begins to speak. "What you see before you are logs of communications from this facility to an unknown location deep in the Gureeg Asteroid Belt. They are heavily encrypted, but we are working on a cypher now. The technicians say it may be decoded within the hour."

Deet Tumarian exclaims, "Are you sure?"

The councilman nods, and many of the representatives begin murmuring to one another under their breath. He continues, "In addition we discovered deposits in an account labeled *contributions* that we have no record of suddenly disappearing. Someone in our hallowed government is colluding with the worst criminal in this solar system. And we need to find him ... now. As such, I am respectfully requesting that you remain here in your offices until we have decoded the messages. We will then meet back here and get to the bottom of this. Do I have your cooperation in this matter?"

The council raises their hands in agreement, save for Faylen and Deet. Faylen stands and says, "Am I a prisoner?"

Reital responds, "No it is j—"

Faylen interrupts, "As I wish to dispel these wild accusations as much as anyone else in this room, I will abide by this request … for one hour! If we do not hear anything back from the intelligence department by then, I will be leaving until tomorrow's session. You may contact me in my office. Is that suitable?"

Reital, sensing Clog's irritation and not wanting to cause any further commotion with the rest of the council, agrees, "I think that is fair. Okay, everyone, this meeting is adjourned for one hour. Please remain in your offices until then, and if we hear something sooner, I will contact you all immediately. Thank you."

As the large doors to the main hall slide open, the members all rise from their chairs and usher out while speaking to one another in hushed tones. The prime minister shoots a stare to Reital before leaving. Faylen's height projects a dominating force as he strides menacingly down the concourse with his long white hair and robes trailing behind him, not uttering a word. Deet Tumarian follows the leader like an obedient pet down the corridor toward their offices. Once they are removed from the other members, the bespectacled man complains to Clog in a high-pitched, shrill voice, "That's it. We're finished! We need to confess."

Clog grabs the small man's shoulder and squeezes it tightly, causing Deet to wince in pain. The tall man stares down at him and whispers in a low and foreboding voice, "Shut your mouth. We don't know what they have. Let me get to my office and see what's going on. If you want to stay alive, keep quiet. Do you understand?"

The diminutive man nods and scurries away. Faylen keys a command into a touch screen by the entrance of his office, and the door quickly slides shut. He crosses to his desk, where he sits and surveys the spacious room. A few paintings adorn the white walls of Clog's office and a large window reveals a panoramic view of the capital city of Solonos. After keying several commands, the display acknowledges that communications are now encrypted, and the window goes from clear to black as the hue of the room dims to red. A holographic image of Warden Braytire Frukas appears in front of him. Faylen Clog pans and says, "Well … where's Luval?"

The warden begins to scream, "I want Dax's head on a platter!"

Clog cuts him off. "Warden, we went over this. We will deal with Dax."

"But he *has* to pay!"

"He's trapped on an asteroid! We'll address that issue later. Where is the prisoner! Is it done?"

Braytire cautions, "Maybe. There was a nasty bit with some Kragors in the Lore Jungle. The problem is the ratings are off the charts. We need to be transparent."

"I don't give a damn about the game. Do you have a body?"

"The remains are being processed now. They should know in an hour."

"If he's still alive, he can't win."

"Prime Minister Clog, even if he survived, which is a big if, judging by the level of destruction, Luval has broken so many rules that he is disqualified and will be terminated on site."

"Make sure it's taken care of. I will deal with things here." He taps the desk forcefully, terminating the image, then sits back in his chair.

Faylen makes another call. A gruff voice comes over the speaker. "This is Dax."

"You didn't need to do that to Frukas' family. He's pissed. He will be a problem."

"Frukas is a fool. He's worthless."

"I don't think Luval's dead yet. We may need to implement the backup plan. Where are the wife and child? Are they there with you?"

"No. The Libertarium executed a raid on my facility and *took* the whore and brat. I thought it was you at first. I got out just in time.

"What!"

"My men on the security force will take care of Drotham, but I hear there's an *issue* with the council. We may need to consider Lieth's termination," schemes Dax.

Clog replies, "I will send word once the council reconvenes," then terminates the call.

He sits back in his chair and stares at the wall. After a moment, he leans forward and slams his hand on the desk. Bowing and shaking his head, the prime minister begins to type on a tablet. Faylen stops and ponders; *it might be time for an exit strategy.* He summons his aide. "Get me a shuttle. Quickly!"

The voice responds over the speaker, "But Councilman Reital put the compound on—"

"As duly elected prime minister of the Rey-Lin system, I am *ordering* you to summon my shuttle for a governmental emergency. Priority one!"

"Do you have a destination?"

Clog shouts irritatingly, "Yes I have a destination! I will tell the pilot. Now get me the damn shuttle!"

The aide stutters as he responds, "Y-yes, sir."

The prime minister hastily shoves the tablet and some other folders into a satchel, then hurries out of his office down the long, high-ceilinged corridor. He turns into a side hallway and climbs some stairs that lead out onto the landing pad positioned on the roof of the government facility. Two armed guards join him as he exits and makes his way across the wind-swept tarmac to a waiting shuttle. Once inside, the politician commands to the pilot, "Out!"

The aviator, surprised by the demand, raises his visor and begins to speak, "Sir I-"

Clog barks in a threatening voice, "This is a priority one emergency mission and *you* don't have clearance. I am commandeering this shuttle …*alone!* Please exit the craft or I will have the guards remove you."

The pilot looks out at the other two men peering in and all shrug at the prime minister's request. The aeronaut gets up and leaves, then

Clog sits down in the pilot's seat and hurriedly preps the craft. As soon as the man exits, the gull wing door swings shut. The black craft unglues itself quickly from the landing pad, and streaks off into the darkening sky with a crack from its powerful beam-drives.

Reital Lieth walks swiftly down the main hallway looking side to side. He stops an aide and inquires, "Where is Prime Minister Clog?"

The aide looks quizzically at the council member and then responds, "Sir, he left in a hurry a short while ago."

"What? He knew the council was on lockdown!"

"He said it was a priority-one mission for the council. I, I—my orders in this matter state I should—"

"Never mind, son. Where did he go?"

"We're not sure. He said the mission was top secret, and he rushed out to his shuttle. He even kicked-out the pilot before taking off quickly, then going orbital. Flight ops lost track after that."

"Lost track?"

"Yes, it seems he disengaged the ship's transponder."

"Did he say when he would be back?"

"No, sir, and also, it was strange that he never left us a flight plan. He just demanded to leave and said it was important state business."

Reital looks down and whispers under his breath, "I knew it."

"Sir?"

"Nothing, son. Please send a communiqué out to the other council members. Tell them I would like to reconvene at oh-nine-hundred Sulimay time and it is a matter of grave importance."

"Yes, sir." The aide then spins and hurries off in the opposite direction.

Reital hurries to his office and shuts the door. He sits behind the desk and contacts the System Guard command.

"This is Councilman Reital Lieth for Commander Duriness."

A voice returns over the com, and then a face appears as a holographic image in front of Reital's desk.

"This is Commander Duriness."

"Commander, this is Undersecretary Reital Lieth of the High Council."

The officer confirms over the speaker, "Yes, sir. What can I do for you?"

"Prime Minister Faylen Clog has left the compound after we issued a lockdown. He has disabled his transponder. I need central command to track the location of his shuttle."

"Will this be a problem? Is his ship dangerous?"

"I don't believe so. Just track him … please. Do not engage. Do you understand?"

The voice over the speaker obeys. "Yes, sir."

As the politician ends the call, he spies his reflection on the smooth black desktop and struggles with the reality that maybe *Faylen* is the traitor. His compassionate mind makes it difficult to comprehend the thought. *Faylen Clog … the prime minister of the High Council. Why?*

MOUNTAIN OF PERIL

Tosin is flying the ship dangerously close to the mountains as he attempts to evade the other ship's and drone's sensors. Yukev, agitated by the proximity to the sheer rock walls, complains, "Damn it, Tosin! Your wife is fine. Do you have a death wish?"

The pilot responds coolly, "You said hug the terrain to stay off radar, right?"

"Yeah, but ..."

"Tiller, you just get those numbers right. Let me fly."

"Sorry. Never seen anyone fly like this. By the way, watch for volcanoes."

"Volcanoes?"

"Yeah, there's two. Looks like the ring's not near either of them, but there are stray vents up here that tend to blow off unexpectedly, so be careful."

Tosin nods. Yukev advises, "Okay, we're ten kilometers back. We will be on them in a matter of minutes."

Major Luval questions, "Are you sure about the distances? It has to be perfect, or it won't work."

Yukev assures, "It's right. Just use the coordinates I gave you. It'll work."

Jenidayah and Zander had become bored and were trying to play a card game but had given up once they got into the Rusage mountain range due to Tosin's erratic maneuvering. She begins to make some small talk. "Well, now that you know about me, what's your story?"

Zander smiles then explains, "Seems we both done got had, miss. I was workin' at a diner on Kree. Nice little place. I liked the people and made a pretty good menu. I was doin' fine, den one day dis man come in and start makin' a big fuss. Gettin' duh customers all scared. I comes out from duh kitchen and he jumps over the counter screamin' he wants everybody's money. He goes n' grabs a ring right off some poor lady's finger. I tells him tuh stop, and he lunges at me. I got a knife in my hand, and as we fall, he lands right on it. I like's to keep my cutlery nice and sharp, and it goes right through dat boy's neck. I tries tuh stop duh bleedin', but he dies right der on duh floh. Next ting I knows, I'm charged with killin' him. Turns out he was some big wig's son. I claim self-defense, but duh trial was a joke, and off I goes to Drotham. I gots an appeal goin', but dey say it will be awhile."

Jenidayah shakes her head. "Hmmph, seems like you got the shaft too."

Yukev, almost falling, climbs down the ladder and braces himself as he makes his way back to the cargo hold. He spies the two crewmembers talking. Zander complains to Yukev that Jenidayah kept winning, and now it's too shaky for him to try to get his money back. Jenidayah barks at the navigator, "What the hell is he doing up there! We had to strap in."

Tiller ducks his head as a container whizzes past him, then yells over the whine of the engines, "I told him to hug the terrain to avoid radar, but … I'm concerned he's actually having too much fun up there. I can't look out the front because I keep getting nauseous."

He stares at the container, which has now wedged itself in a corner, then continues, "We're ten clicks out. It has to happen perfectly or the plan won't work. Jen, he wants you to operate the hook for this. Zander, man the guns. Ultan is ready to broadcast, but they want us to play out the game for some stupid reason."

Jenidayah replies, "Yeah, if he doesn't *kill* us first," pointing forward at the flight deck.

She and Zander unclip their harnesses and shakily walk to the gun stations at both ends of the cargo hold, and strap in again. Jenidayah informs, "Tell the flyboy we're ready."

Yukev smiles and heads back up to the flight deck. As he tops out the stairs, he recoils at the sight out of the front canopy. He yelps at the pilot, "Whoa! That was too close, man!"

Luval seems quite amused and replies, "I figured out how to get the ship to sync the display with my visor. It's working like a charm."

The pasty navigator's skin looks even whiter than normal. He straps in and gazes out the front canopy, petrified by the pilot's skill.

Luval asks, "Distance?"

Tiller replies, "Five kilometers. Do you have to fly like this?"

The number eight ship is a kilometer from the steel plated ring and is lining up to drop the Drothamae into the aperture. The pursuing number four shuttle dips underneath the other vessel, launches its harpoon to grab the ball, but misses. The defender deploys air brakes and slows quickly while the challenger races forward, and begins to come around for a second attempt. The number eight vessel unloads a flurry of laser fire on the assailant, hitting one of the engine pods. The injured number four craft begins belching smoke and falls away, then crashes onto a rocky slope with a large explosion.

The number ten ship, which has been watching from a distance, swoops in and executes the same move. This time the new aggressor's grappling claw finds its mark, then fires a streak of light that severs the number eight ship's cable. The large metal ball falls loose and is swept up into the recess of the other craft which accelerates out from underneath, then banks hard to the left while laying down cover fire as it bolts away.

Tosin and Tiller are watching the dog fight on a screen in the cockpit, and the pilot comments, "That guy's good."

Yukev agrees, "Yeah, it's not gonna be easy getting it from them."
"Time's running out. We need to get up to them. Are you ready?"
"Yep."
Tosin orders, "Now!"
Tiller punches a key, and their shanghaied guard ship's color changes from red to charcoal gray with the number two displayed on the wings of the ship. It pops up out of a canyon directly behind the number ten ship. Zander focuses the cannons on the prison shuttle and discharges several volleys, which rock the aircraft. The explosive metal sphere jars loose and begins sagging underneath the speeding vessel.

Two referee ships suddenly drop down behind their battered shuttle and commence firing. Tosin evades the incoming barrage, and in a daring maneuver, flips the ship upside down, then quickly brings it in underneath the number ten craft. Zander slices the cable with a beam from the underside gun turret, then Jenidayah snags the ball with their grappler as it falls away. The Drothamae—with the LED readout on the side of metal sphere counting down the final thirty seconds before it detonates—plops into the indentation of their still inverted craft. Tosin guns the engines and pulls out in front of the other shuttle before executing a barrel roll in the opposite direction. One of the referee ships clips the number ten vessel, and both loose control before careening into a mountain wall followed by an immense blast.

Tiller types in commands on his keyboard, and the heads-up display confirms a round metal aperture with bright red lights encircling it in the side of a rock wall half a kilometer in front of them. The ball's display starts to blink as it shows only ten seconds left before detonation.

The pilot beckons, "Jen?"
Jenidayah confirms, "Target lock. Bomb away!"
Luval pulls back hard on the yoke, and the shuttle climbs vertically up the rock face. The ball launches and slams squarely into

the nulling ring. The lights go green, and the timer stops with only one second to go. The other referee ship continues trailing them, and unleashes a withering salvo of pulse cannon fire at them. Jenidayah, barely able to hold on because of Tosin's back and forth dodging, manages to get from the grappling station over to the other firing yoke. She swivels the gun turret to begin assisting Zander who has been returning fire at the pursuing military vehicle.

Reital and the rest of the council are all watching on a large screen in the main chamber. He questions, "Why are they still firing? Get me Braytire Frukas … now!"

The screen abruptly changes to an image of a woman with dark skin underneath long dreads of white cornrow hair and light blue-gray eyes surrounded by a sharp face.

"Hello. Good people of the Rey-Lin system, sorry to interfere in this exciting game, but my name is Na'edra Lynn. I am the leader of a group called the Libertarium. We have been tracking the rampant corruption of the High Council for some time now. Your prime minister is a traitor! He has been working in collusion with Maytor Dax. Here is the proof." She taps a tablet she is holding, and an intercepted recording of Clog and Dax is played.

"Major Luval was a perfect scapegoat. Now you get to continue your operations and the High Council looks like they have driven you away. Everybody wins."

"Fine, Clog, but you still owe me—and make sure Frukas deals with Luval. I don't want any loose ends."

"What about the family?"

"I have the whore and brat for leverage. Once he's gone, I will end them."

She taps the tablet again, looks up, and summarizes, "Tosin Luval was framed. We have successfully rescued his wife and child, Desiree and Robey Luval. We also destroyed the Daxian gang hideout in the Gureeg Asteroid Belt but believe he has escaped. It's up to you now to right this wrong. Free Luval, bring Prime Minister Clog to justice, and purge your government of the spies and moles that are crippling it. Na'edra … out."

The screen goes back to the chase still unfolding on Drotham. Reital is staring at the screen and demanding answers. "Where's the warden? Call off that ship!"

An aide responds, "We can't locate the warden, and they are saying the pursuit ship is not responding. Command believes they're Dax's men … mercenaries hired to kill Luval."

"I want Commander Duriness to dispatch System Guard personnel to find Clog. And issue an order to the prison guards to assist Major Luval by shooting down that ship!"

Yukev yells over the din of the whining engines, "Well, we did it. But these bastards seem like sore losers."

"They're Dax's men. They don't care," points out Luval. "Jen? What's going on back there?"

Jenidayah yells, "That isn't a normal ship! They've got heavy shielding. Our weapons don't seem to be affecting them."

Tosin barks, "Okay, everybody, strap in tight. It's going to get bumpy." As he lowers his visor, he turns toward Tiller and comments, "You may want to close your eyes."

Yukev tightens his harness and squints his eyes shut while he begins whispering one of his family's old prayers. Luval hears him and makes a slight smile and calls over to his navigator, "You know what they say. Don't pray for yourself … pray for the pilot."

Tiller stops opens his eyes to see the ship heading straight at a mountain and shuts them tight again and begins praying faster. Luval adds speed and begins a death-defying run several meters above the rapidly changing terrain below, dodging and turning the ship as if it is a toy. The mercenary ship is falling behind and then clips the side of an outcropping but is still in pursuit. Both craft descend into a deep, long trench. Luval throttles up for a final burst of speed, then follows it by fully deploying the air brakes. The ship's flaps are fully extended as it begins climbing the sheer wall at the end of the trench. The rogue shuttle attempts the same maneuver but is too slow and slams into the rock wall, creating an explosion that reaches up and shakes the escaping shuttle violently. Warning beeps begin to chime in the cockpit, and Tiller opens his eyes and balks in disbelief, "We're alive!"

The pilot warns, "We took a hit. Go back and check on Jen and Zander. I think there's a fire back there."

The navigator undoes his harness and leaps out of the seat. As he nears the cargo hold, he can hear Jenidayah shouting.

"Get another fire suppressor! This one's almost out."

Zander limps toward the other extinguisher, but he is bleeding from his forehead and having trouble seeing. He stumbles and begins to fall when Tiller catches him and reassures him, "I gotcha, buddy. I gotcha. What happened?"

"Sumfin' done blow'd up. Next ting we tryin' ta stop duh fire. Den duh ship was heavin' and hoein', an I done got hit wit a piece o' scrap."

Jenidayah bellows, "Tiller! Get over here now!"

Tiller helps Zander onto the floor, and the dark-skinned man beams a bright white smile. "You best hep dat girl oh she gonna swat you one ... heh heh."

"Okay just be still. We made it. We're gonna be okay," Yukev reassures.

The navigator helps Zander over to a bench and lies him down, then straps him and props his head up with a towel. He grabs an extinguisher off the wall and hurries toward the blaze in the rear of the hold.

"Nice shot with the ball, girl," he says, complimenting Jenidayah as he begins unloading the retardant on the fire next to her.

"Took you long enough," she retorts as her canister runs dry and she throws it aside.

"You know, you might want to look into some anger-management classes for that temp—"

"Oh screw you! What are you—my shrink? Just because you can fix crap doesn't give you the right to lecture me."

"Damn, girl … never mind," Yukev ends the conversation as the last of the flames fizzle out. He places the extinguisher on the floor and hurries back up to the flight deck.

After climbing back into his seat, he turns to the pilot and bemoans, "You know, she really is a bitch. Damn … I mean we just survived this mess, and she's back there as angry as a junkyard mutt."

"She had a hard life. She'll be fine when this is all over. And … she stuck the ball. Can't be too mad at her," Tosin reminds Tiller.

A voice comes through on the speaker in the cockpit. "Major Tosin Luval? This is Reital Lieth of the High Council. Can you here me, sir?"

Tosin looks over and comments to Yukev before answering, "Okay, here we go," then pushes the broadcast switch on the com. "Yes, Councilman. This is Major Luval."

"I would first like to offer our sincerest apologies for this situation."

"Situation? Is that what you are spinning this as, sir?"

"Major … I understand you are upset, but please listen. We have guard ships on the way to accompany you back to the pris—"

"What! Hell no. We're plotting a course for orbit!"

"Uh okay. I didn't realize you had that capability in a prison shuttle."

Tosin nods over to Yukev. The navigator types in a command, and the nose of the ship turns bright red again, indicating that the nano-wrap paint has been deactivated.

The pilot replies, "We needed to appropriate another vehicle after the Lore Jungle incident and discovered some stealth technology at an outpost."

"Mmmm … very enterprising indeed, sir. All warrants against

you have been retracted. We will contact a Guard space cruiser to meet you in orbit. Do you require any medical attention?"

Luval looks at Yukev, who puts up one finger and mouths the name Zander.

"Yes, Councilman, we have one injury, not life-threatening though. Also, the rest of my crew is to be pardoned … completely."

"Well, we will have to rev—"

"Sir, you will honor this request, or I will notify the Libertarium that you are wrongfully holding two of their people against their will. Do you really want a system-wide revolution after this mess?"

There is a pause in the communication, and then Reital acquiesces. "By order of the High Council of Rey-Lin, your crew is pardoned. I will await your arrival on Sulimay to finalize the details. Lieth out."

Luval glances at Yukev, who has both arms in the air and is whispering, "Yes!"

Tosin then focuses his attention on prepping the ship for the orbital rendezvous when a beeping sound begins. He shoots a sideways glare at Yukev, who is already keying commands on his keyboard as a new holo-image appears in between them. He confirms his suspicions. "Bogey! Thirty thousand and climbing. Tracking at two-nine-hundred degrees."

Tosin shouts in his com, "Jen!"

Jen's voice returns over the speaker. "What!"

"Secure Zander and get on the aft pulse cannon. We have visitors." The pilot's voice trails off.

"Not again! Zander says he'll make you your favorite dish if we don't die," says the woman.

Tosin and Yukev turn and look at each other, and the navigator says, "Nothing with a face. I can't eat animals, man!"

The pilot radios, "We'll discuss the menu later. Jen, are you set? Because they're closing fast."

"Set."

A voice comes over their communication system. "Major Luval! We are tracking a ship approaching you at a high rate of speed."

The officer replies, "Yeah, we see him, but we're still eighty thousand below orbit."

"We requested they identify but no response. We consider them a threat."

Yukev yells, "They've got a missile lock!"

Tosin comments calmly, "Deploy countermeasures. Jen?"

"Two missiles away," yelps the navigator.

Her voice comes back, "There's two of them. Coming up fast. I wanna wait until they get close to each other."

"Jen, shoot the damn things now", demands the pilot.

"Just a little more …"

"Jen!" screams the pilot.

A long stream of blue-white energy intersects both missiles at the same time and a blast confirms their destruction. Another large beam of red light rains down from the sky above and obliterates the pursuing ship.

Tosin and Yukev shout, "Yeah!"

Tosin continues, "Nice shot, Jen."

"I'm going to check on Zander. Can you please keep it smooth?"

The pilot chuckles and then responds, "No promises. But I'll try.

Two System Guard ships appear on either side of their windows, and both dip their wings quickly, indicating they aren't a threat.

After being escorted into space, the battered red referee ship docks inside a System Guard cruiser in orbit above Drotham. Medical technicians walk down the ramp of the vehicle with Zander on a stretcher while Tosin, Yukev, and Jenidayah watch.

Jenidayah starts, "They're going to debrief us for days."

"Well, we've got nothing to lie about. It was all broadcast on video." Yukev holds up a tablet replaying the final seconds of the game. "I shoulda put down a bet." The three begin to laugh.

Tosin notices the guards starting to approach them and remarks, "You are the best crew I've ever worked with. Thank you so much for helping my family and me. Jen … I am so—"

Jenidayah puts her hand to his mouth, "Tosin, stop. I'm glad I didn't kill you at the depot." They all chuckle again before she continues. "You told us to trust you, so we did. You pulled it off, and … you are one *damn* good pilot, flyboy." The woman turns to Yukev and adds, "And you," as she points a figure at the waifish redhead. "You are scary. I better not find out you hacked my social account or your dead!"

GAME OVER

Desiree had only been to Ultan once many years ago when it was still rebuilding from the tragedy of the collapsed cities. It seems … different. Stronger. Her son gazes around in awe at the ceilings and rows of buildings. He remarks excitedly, "Mom! I can't believe we're underground. And it feels nice! It must be five hundred degrees on the surface. How do they do it?"

"I'm not sure, honey. Something to do with how they channel and vent the heat for energy."

"Is it safe?"

Na'edra walks up to them and puts her hand on Robey's head and reassures the young boy, "Of course it's safe! We have lived here for almost a thousand years. And now with the new earthquake measures in place, it's even better than ever. Maybe your mom will take you to the waterfalls. You won't even notice you're a kilometer under ground."

Desiree smiles at him and then looks up at her. She begins, "Na'edra, we can't th—"

"Stop, child," the woman comforts. "Dax is a horrible man, but we needed your husband to win the game to maximize the effect. We were never going to be able to broadcast to as wide an audience as at the end of Drothamae. Let's just say his winning was a little extra public relations initiative."

"Have you heard from him? When can we see him?"

"He is being debriefed at System Guard central command on Seltuvay. Then he will be sent to the High Council on Sulimay. There is a great deal the council wants to know."

"What about those bastards Dax and Clog?"

The dark-skinned woman bows her head and pauses before speaking. "We thought Dax was killed in the raid when we freed you, but sensors show he escaped using a shifting pod. The coordinates were scrambled, so he could be anywhere right now. But we've rounded up the rest of his cartel and shut down his operations, so it will be difficult for him to hide for very long. At least in this system."

"And Clog?"

"The ex-prime minister is another story. It turns out he was aided by a lower council member named Deet Tumarian, who is now undergoing interrogation. We have a theory as to where he is hiding and hope to arrest him shortly. As soon as Major Luval completes his debriefing, the System Guard will escort you to Sulimay to meet him. I hear there is going to be a grand ceremony in his honor. But for now, please rest and enjoy our world as a guest of honor. After all, your husband is considered a great hero around here, and one of—if not the greatest—Drothamae champions of all time."

Desiree holds her son, smiles, and then softly says, "Thank you so much," as tears begin welling up in her eyes.

After the planetary journey from Drotham, and two days on Seltuvay for debriefing, Tosin departs the System Guard heavy cruiser in orbit over Sulimay in a shuttlecraft that dips down into the atmosphere and heads to the High Council's government complex in Solonos. The government facility on Sulimay looks starkly different than System Guard command. All the structures use white concrete, stone, and glass instead of the dark gray, heavily reinforced *steelcrete* used by the military. Tosin begins to relax for the first time in months as he appraises the view, noticing the perfect alignment of the trees in front of fences and walls covered by shrubs and flora. The shuttle circles the rooftop of the main building and settles firmly on the tarmac. The gull-wing door of the ship unfolds upward, and Tosin, now in his dress uniform, exits the craft. Commander Loland

Duriness and his aide stand in front of a complement of soldiers and greet him with a collective salute. Duriness offers, "Major. I am sorry. This wasn't —"

Tosin cuts him off. "Commander, can we get on with this? I want to see my wife."

Duriness accedes, "Of course. Men! Escort detail … ho!"

The soldiers salute, fall into information around him, and all march over to a lift at the edge of the landing pad. Once at the principle level, the elevator door opens and they head down a corridor toward the main hall. The clapping and cheering staff and military personnel who have assembled along the passageway to greet him, surprises the major. The escort promenades by and continues to the council chamber. As he enters the grand room, Tosin observes the insignia of individual planets of the Rey-Lin system on tapestries that cascade down the granite walls on each side. The marble floor beneath his feet and large curtains behind the councilmembers grand bench bears the familiar emblem of the solar system—two suns with a triangle intersecting them. Reital Lieth sits in the center with the remaining council members on either side of him, all in high-back chairs, looking down at the major from behind the long semicircular desk. The councilman raises his hand above his shoulder, and the military escort leaves the room. Commander Duriness moves off to the side and sits behind a credenza. The room becomes quiet as Lieth scans his notes, then rises and proceeds to a podium on the right side of the large stone desk before speaking. "Major Luval, on behalf of the entire Rey-Lin system, I thank you for your service and am deeply sorry for the terrible injustice you and your family have endured. Consider this your government's formal pardon for this unfortunate misunderstanding. Also, the council has suggested, and Commander Duriness has agreed, that you should be promoted to sub-commander of the System Guard."

The crowd applauds and cheers with several hoots and whistles emanating from the group as well. Reital claps slowly, stands back from the rostrum, and motions with his arm for Luval to join him. Tosin walks up some steps at the side of the stage and shakes the new prime minister's hand, then turns to the podium. He pauses for a moment, staring out at the large group of people amassed in the hall before beginning his speech. "Members of the council, distinguished guests, and my fellow brothers and sisters of the guard, I have served for over twenty years and devoted my life to upholding our law. I am thankful that this matter has been resolved and believe many good things will come from this incident."

Reital surveys the crowd and notices many smiles on the faces of the audience.

The major continues, "The interim prime minister is correct that we will need to be vigilant and progressive in governing moving forward. To that end, I would like to make a formal request that the Libertarium be granted amnesty, and given full diplomatic privileges, *including* a seat on the High Council."

A subtle gasp comes over the crowd. After a moment, Reital turns to the other council members who look at one other, then nod in approval. He steps up next to Tosin and issues his first decree. "As acting prime minister of the High Council of Rey-Lin, I hereby authorize that the Libertarium be fully recognized by our government. We offer them full amnesty and request they select an ambassador to join our council."

Tosin smiles at Reital and surveys the crowd, which is again applauding in approval. The officer waits for the congregation to quite down and then continues.

"Lastly, while the High Council's offer is flattering, I have decided to resign my commission so that I may be with my wife and son."

Luval's family emerges from the side of the stage, and Robey runs up and hugs his leg while Desiree embraces her husband and bestows a kiss to him. She pulls back for a moment, and then he hugs her tightly while she whispers in his ear, "I missed you, my love. Did you mean it? Is it really over?"

Tosin stares deeply as their green eyes meet, and confirms, "It's over, honey. I'm done. Let's go home."

He bends down, grabs his son, and hoists him up before turning out to the audience to announce, "Thank you all and be well."

The family exits the stage to a standing ovation. Reital walks alongside Tosin and comments, "Nice speech, Major. You might want to think about entering politics."

Tosin and Desiree collectively answer, "*No*," before smiling and laughing.

As they walk down corridor, his now-famous crew greets him. Jenidayah, in a colorful ensemble, is the first to speak. "I take back every bad thing I ever said about you flyboy. Na'edra was almost in tears when you requested inclusion of the Libertarium. They're scrambling around on Ultan trying to figure out who's going to represent them."

Yukev Tiller shakes the major's hand. "So you're really retiring? Man, that's a shock."

"I think I've had enough excitement for one life," Luval replies. "So what about you?"

The lanky man with pasty skin informs, "They freed me but told me I can't touch a computer unless I work for them. I said no thanks. I'm shifting back to the Aldo system. They say I still have family there. And Major, I gotta mention one last thing. Honestly … I think it was more than just luck *or* your crazy flying. Maybe there really is some *thing* looking out for us. But I still ain't prayin' five times a day."

They all laugh for a moment.

Zander, his dark skin a stark contrast to the bright white coat he is wearing, shakes Desiree's hand. "Yo man was duh best, dawlin'. Nevuh seen nuffin' like him flyin' dat machine. Like he's possessed o' sumfin'."

Tosin points at his head, "Zander, what's with the hat?"

"Oh dey axe me what I can do 'sides shoot, and I says I can cook.

Rustled up some grub foh some uh duh impohtant fellas. Next ting I knows … I's cookin' foh duh big wigs nah."

The major holds on to his beloved wife and then addresses them. "I said this before but again … I can't thank you all enough for helping me. I'm sorry I flew a little crazy, and if any of you ever make it to Flon D'Mar, you're always welcome in our home."

Reital interrupts, "Speaking of which, you have a shuttle to catch. The space transport in orbit is leaving at fourteen hundred sharp. So we need to be going."

Luval takes turns embracing everyone and takes a parting shot at Jenidayah. "They wanted me to run for office, but I think you're the better candidate."

"Oh no. Not me," declines the woman warrior. "They say the pen is mightier, but my sword is still sharper—thank you very much. Besides, Na'edra wants me close to her. She *says* she wants me as one of her personal guards. I think the lady just wants to keep an eye on me," she muses.

The major smiles before he, his family and the prime minister move down the hall and into an elevator that brings them back up to the rooftop tarmac. A waiting shuttle is poised for takeoff. As they get to the edge of the craft's ramp, the prime minister queries, "So now what will you do?"

Luval replies, "Go fishing, raise my family, and probably write a book about this," as he hugs his wife and son.

Lieth smiles and pats him on the shoulder. "You deserve it. But we could always use a—"

The major cuts him off before the shuttle's ramp begins to close. "Respectfully, Prime Minister, I'm done. But please contact me if you ever find any of those bastards."

The politician nods, then steps back from the ship, observing as it rises slowly off the landing pad. Reital shields his face from the swirling wind around the vehicle as it gains altitude and then bolts off into the bright blue sky.

EPILOGUE

The spaceport on Kree is old. The walls need new paint. There are plans to expand it to handle the increased capacity the facility is experiencing, but for now, it's just crowded and dirty. Video screens on the walls broadcast news commentators reviewing the shocking revelations of treason by the former prime minister and other government officials as well as the spectacular finish of the latest Drothamae competition. The images of the faces splattered all over the solar system have necessitated Faylen Clog to change his appearance. With his long white mane and moustache shaved off, he now sports a bald scalp and shaven face hidden under a gray, hooded shirt. The disgraced politician sits alone at a table topped with a glass of darkish brown liquid. He stares down at a boarding pass he has just purchased using some of the fake credentials leftover from his time serving in the intelligence wing of the System Guard. The journey will be long but a good way to disappear and try to start over in a nearby system. He downs the drink, which leaves a ring of froth around his mouth. A friendly announcement from a soothing woman's voice can be heard echoing through the halls from the speakers in the ceiling. "Passengers for the *Star Liner* to the Aldo system may begin boarding at hangar eighteen in ten minutes." After a short, pensive moment, he wipes his face with the sleeve of his sweater, stands, and slowly walks down the hallway, melding into the sea of beings at the bustling installation.

Braytire Frukas has just finished secretly meeting his family in a restaurant on Seltuvay. His brother, sharing the same golden locks as he, walks down a side alleyway and pleads, "Bray, they are looking for you everywhere. Why don't you just surrender and tell them what happened. This wasn't your fault."

The ex-warden balks, "He killed Father! He *has* to pay. If I come forward now, I will never be able to find him."

"Who? Dax? They say he's dead. They found the body in that shifting pod."

"No. He got away. I saw a copy of the logs. He made it out. I still have some friends, and I think I know where he is. I am going to kill that man myself!"

"Well, be careful," the brother warns.

"I'll be fine, but will you be okay?"

"They confiscated your estate, but we are staying with my wife's relatives. I'm not worried for us. It's you they're after."

Frukas puts a hand on his brother's shoulder and declares, "I will contact you when it's done. Maybe then I will come in."

They embrace before Braytire retreats down the alley and fades into the night.

Tosin, Desiree, and their son, Robey, step off the transport after their long passage, and smell the distinctly salty air. Even though they are several kilometers from the ocean, the aroma reminds them they are finally home on Flon D'Mar. Desiree becomes emotional and hugs Tosin tightly.

An officer walks over to them and introduces himself. "Major Luval, sir. Excuse me. My name is Lieutenant Raylor, and I've been assigned to accompany you back to your home, sir."

"It's nice to meet you, son, but that won't be necessary."

"I'm sorry, sir. I'm under orders," the officer insists.

"Well, I wouldn't want you to get in trouble. We all know what that can lead to," Tosin offers cheekily.

Raylor requests, "Permission to speak freely, sir."

"Granted."

"Sir, we all thought this whole thing—your conviction—was a crock. We never believed what they said about you. My CO said he served with you. He told me stories about you. Said you were a straight-up top notch guy."

The junior officer looks at the other guards in his escort, and they all nod in agreement. He adds, "And for the record, sir, a bunch of us made a ton of money off you." He and the others begin to laugh.

Luval speaks in a serious tone. "I'm glad my misfortune brought you all such good luck."

The officer and soldiers quickly stop chuckling, and the lieutenant apologizes, "Sir, we meant no dis—"

Tosin starts to laugh and quips, "So what's my cut?"

The military complement is stunned into silence before Desiree lightly punches her husband on the arm. "Honey, stop teasing them. They're trying to thank you." She begins to giggle.

The group bursts into laughter, and Tosin pats the officer on the shoulder before inquiring, "So what's a guy gotta do to get a lift around here?"

The men quiet down, and the lieutenant orders them into formation around the family before stating more formally, "Right this way, sir."

The group heads toward a sleek, black ground shuttle, and once seated, the craft hovers up off the ground and darts away toward the ocean.

Maytor Dax—now disguised with a wig and eye patch—sits at a table of a seedy tavern located in the backwater and bombed-out province of Tal Rutette on Kree. The acrid smell of frying meat and pipe smoke permeates the small, dimly lit pub, and there are only a few patrons in the saloon. With most of his thugs either dead or locked up and his illegal empire destroyed, the obese crime lord is hiding from authorities now on a relentless crusade to apprehend him. The Quantum Matter Shifting pod got him off the asteroid, but he didn't have time to program it for an interstellar jump to the neighboring Aldo solar system. Dax keeps a private lair on a planet there as a failsafe. The criminal's contact said to meet him here, then he would take him to an illegal pod so Maytor could escape the Rey-Lin system. It has been an hour, and Dax is becoming both impatient and paranoid. He looks around, and thinks; *Five more minutes, and I'm out of here.*

Braytire Frukas sits in a secluded booth on the opposite side of the establishment, spying the fat gangster. He keys in a command on a tablet and observes as Dax looks down at his com device, eyeing the message Braytire has just sent. *Proof!* The money he spent on Boss Takahata's informant was worth it. The disgraced warden confirms this is the man who stole his father's life. He holds up a small dart gun weapon—also a little present from Takahata—, fires it quickly, then puts the piece down on the seat next to him. Dax swats the back of his neck, thinking an insect has bitten him. The tiny projectile is only the size of a grain of rice and falls to the floor, but the deadly poison it has delivered begins to course through the veins of the grotesque man's body. Braytire rises from the booth, quietly walks past the murderous thug, and exits the pub. Several moments later, the plump criminal starts to convulse uncontrollably, then grabs at his chest before falling out of the chair. A young barmaid runs to him and observes white foam oozing out of his mouth. The crime lord, now suffering a fatal heart attack from the special toxin—bioengineered spewcifically for his genes—that attacks his body at the cellular level, utters a final death rattle. While the young waitress and some patrons look over him, Maytor Dax expires on the floor of the dimly lit tavern.

Braytire walks several paces, pulls a hood over his blond hair, and pauses to observe the emergency vehicles with blaring sirens arriving at the bar behind him. He whispers under his breath, "This was for you, Father. You are avenged," as he vanishes into the night mist of a dark, foggy street.

THE END

ABOUT THE AUTHOR

Eddie Ruzzi is a writer, musician, and producer originally from Atlantic City, New Jersey, now living in Los Angeles, California. He studied at Interlochen Arts Academy and Berklee College of Music and currently works as a sound editor for TV and Film. Along with a soon-to-be-released music CD, this is the first in a series of novels and screenplays he is involved in.

www.ingramcontent.com/pod-product-compliance
Lightning Source LLC
Chambersburg PA
CBHW021200110726
47900CB00002B/663